Beyond the Crimson Skies

Kendo was looking for salvation as well as retribution. Of these two, retribution was the simpler to exact. Losing Frank Pierce's horse herd to raiding gunmen had not been his fault, but it was bound to ruin Kendo's reputation which had already been severely darkened by past failure.

Left alone and afoot on the open plains by treacherous companions, he needed to track down the outlaws and recapture the horses, the sale of which Pierce was banking on to save his small ranch. That alone was a vast challenge and Kendo couldn't know how much worse it could get before he encountered the beautiful woman who was intent on building an outlaw empire in the far country.

By the same author

Devil's Canyon
Drifter's Revenge
West of Tombstone
Gunsmoke Mountain
On the Wapiti Range
Rolling Thunder
The Bounty Killer
Six Days to Sundown
Saddle Tramps
The Shadow Riders
The Outpost

Beyond the Crimson Skies

Owen G. Irons

ROBERT HALE · LONDON

First published in Great Britain 2009

ISBN 978-0-7090-8748-9

Robert Hale Limited
Clerkenwell House
Clerkenwell Green
London EC1R 0HT

www.halebooks.com

Typeset by
Derek Doyle & Associates, Shaw Heath
Printed and bound in Great Britain by
CPI Antony Rowe, Chippenham and Eastbourne

ONE

The sky was on fire and the world was growing dark. The sun was not dying without a whimper. It threw angry confused colors against the clouds, complaining as the far mountains sucked it down to wither and wane behind their towering, snow-capped peaks.

Kendo was not going down without a fight either; he had it in mind to stain the earth with the dark crimson of the traitors' blood.

He rode on, the hoofs of his horse making only muted, seemingly distant sounds against the muddy, buffalo-grass-dappled soil underfoot. There was not a light to be seen anywhere across the long plains. Few settlers had even tried to make a start on this remote high prairie, fewer still had made a go of it. There were no settlements that Kendo was aware of.

Yet on this night, as much as he wished to avoid civilization and its watchful eyes, he wished that he might somehow find a place to rest.

Where he might find someone with enough skill to draw the bullet from his back.

It had promised to be a tough job to begin with. Frank Pierce was the boss's name. He had it in mind to drive a herd of fifty horses out of Cheyenne to Drew Link's new DL ranch along the Idaho line. Good stock was still hard to come by in the north country, but Pierce had them in abundance; Link had none, and his cattle ranch was not going to succeed without them. Link knew Frank Pierce from some previous dealings and he had written to Pierce for help, promising to pay top dollar for saddle horses, even if they were only half broken.

Things began to fall apart almost immediately. Frank Pierce was no longer a young man, and he had gotten himself thrown by an ornery bronc and broken his hip as a result. Frank had two sons, but the older, Marcus, was only fifteen, Frank was not willing to let him try to ramrod a rough crew of men on a 300-mile drive. He was less willing to let Drew Link down. They had a deal, and Frank Pierce had given his word.

'Kendo,' Pierce had said from his bed, 'it's up to you. Link needs those ponies bad. I need the money.

Counting on this sale in advance, I have over-extended myself buying those Herefords. The horses I don't need are grazing on the grass the Herefords will need when they get here. I've got to drive this herd through to Idaho Territory, or. . . .' The old man's watery eyes briefly turned away. 'I need to have those horses pushed to Drew Link's ranch.'

'I understand,' Kendo said sympathetically. 'But why me, Mr Pierce? You have older hands who have been working for you a lot longer.'

'Yes, and some of them have been working for me long enough to expose their shortcomings,' Pierce answered sharply. His hands, resting on top of the blue coverlet tightened a little. 'Just do it, Kendo. There'll be a bonus in it for you.'

Pierce offered Kendo six men for the job, but Kendo bargained him up to eight. It was a long and dangerous drive across hostile territory and he wanted as many sure guns as he could take along. Six hands should be enough to handle the herd, but Kendo wanted two men with keen eyes for outriders, their only task to prevent raiders from hitting them. Fifty saddle-broken horses were worth much in this country at that time. Two extra riders were not that much to ask to prevent Pierce from losing his fortune on the hoof.

Kendo walked from the shadows of the house on

to the front porch of the big white house, looking toward the sun as it fell blazing toward the western horizon. He crouched down, tipped back his hat and pondered.

First, he needed men who were good with horses, and he had a few in mind. The Collier brothers up from Kansas had both been wranglers on a Texas ranch. When the last cattle herd had been driven to the railhead at Wichita, the two blond brothers had taken their pay and kept riding – north to Wyoming, claiming they had spent enough of their lives already looking at the rear ends of cattle.

Hatha, he also wanted on the crew. A Bannock Indian, he was solitary and silent unless someone made mention of the Nez Perce, which tribe he hated with a ferocity he never fully explained. After fifteen years among the whites, Hatha still rode without a saddle, with only a striped blanket thrown over his paint pony's back. It was his third paint pony. Hatha said he did not trust a horse with only one color. Again, he never explained if this was spiritual, tribal or just a personal quirk.

After these three the choice became more difficult. There were men who were good at their jobs but with a tendency to be bunkhouse brawlers. Kendo wanted no trouble within their ranks along the trail. There were others who were frankly too old to ride 300 miles without growing weary, as handy as they were on the home ranch, There were a couple, like Frank Pierce's own sons who were simply too young and inexperienced.

Kendo rose and made his way toward the bunkhouse where smoke rose lazily from the iron stovepipe to blend with the settling gloom of twilight. He continued to turn the problem over in his mind as he walked past a startled cottontail rabbit which bounded away from his boots.

The truth was there were not eight men he fully trusted. Perhaps not even six.

Men came and went. Where they drifted in from was often anyone's guess. No one dug deeply into a man's past this far west. If a hand did his work and caused no trouble, that was good enough. And all a rancher could expect. There were no schoolboys on the Wyoming range – nor would they have lasted long.

No, these men had calluses, spoke slowly and carefully, kept to themselves and took great care of their guns. Kendo knew none of them well, any more than they knew him or his own background. It was just as well.

Entering the bunkhouse, Kendo found most of the men sitting around the dinner table, smoking after their meals had been finished. Dinner had been beef, beans and fried potatoes as it was nearly every night except Sundays when Cooky made fried chicken for them. No one ever complained about the monotony of the meals, it was a better situation than most of them had been in for a long time as far as eating and sleeping out of the weather went. Eyes lifted to the door as Kendo entered.

Rex McColl was standing, his arms folded, leaning against the far wall. The narrow wrangler wore a thin black mustache and a constant half-smile of scorn as if he felt himself superior to every other man on the ranch, and had only landed among them due to circumstances. His friend, Charlie Weeks sat on a bunk nearby, cleaning his pistol. Neither young nor old, the yellow-haired man considered himself a crack shot. He burned dozens of practise rounds through his .44 daily.

Facing these two was Bo Chandler. His dark eyes shifted slowly toward Kendo. Chandler was a big man with sloppy appearing muscles; but Kendo knew there was strength beneath the apparent flab on his shoulders. Chandler considered himself to be ranch foreman although Frank Pierce had never assigned him the job.

These three Kendo had no liking for. They had ridden in together at about the same time Kendo had arrived. From where, he could not guess, but you could almost smell trouble on their backtrail. Bo Chandler ambled over to where Kendo stood, planting himself directly in front of – and too close to – Kendo.

'The boys want to know if the drive's still on now that the old man's broke his hip.'

'It is,' Kendo told him, not backing away from Bo Chandler. 'Mr Pierce has put me in charge of the drive. Wants me to pick out seven men to ride with me.'

Bo Chandler frowned. 'Why you?'

'I don't know. Why don't you go over and ask him?' Kendo went on, speaking up so that every man could hear him. 'Come morning let's start pushing all the ponies into the corral. If you can't get them all, that's all right. The boss wants fifty head for sure, though. That's what he's promised to deliver to Drew Link over in Idaho. Any pony that doesn't look quite fit, leave it behind. Same with any that have forgotten their manners.' He looked steadily at Bo Chandler.

'We don't want any troublemakers along on the drive.'

'Who's going?' Aaron Collier asked from his place at the table.

'You are, and your brother.' Kendo glanced at Billy Collier who nodded, sipped at his coffee and exchanged a glance with his older brother. 'I'd like you to travel with us, Darcy,' Kendo said, to an old trailsman who wore a fringed buckskin shirt and faded blue jeans.

'Kinda old for this, isn't he?' Bo Chandler asked, as he turned to study the lanky man with the long graying hair.

'Only if he thinks he is,' Kendo answered, but Darcy Pitt had already nodded his agreement.

'Who else?' Rex McColl asked, still leaning lazily against the wall.

'I want Hatha with us – anyone seen him?'

'The Indian's not much for socializing,' Darcy Pitt drawled. 'He's probably around. As you know, he usually sleeps out.'

'What about me?' Bo Chandler said belligerently. 'You still need three men. Why not me, Rex and Charlie Weeks here?'

Kendo considered matters. He did not trust those three and didn't wish to ride a long trail with the contrary Chandler. Neither did he think it was a good idea for them to be left to watch the ranch with the few men remaining and Frank Pierce laid up in bed. There was no sense in antagonizing Chandler any further. He nodded his reluctant assent.

'All right,' he finally agreed. He warned Bo, 'Just don't forget who's in charge, Bo, or I'll send you packing.'

Bo Chandler opened his mouth to retort, but he said nothing. Still, a nasty gleam lingered in his black eyes. He nodded, turned away and went back to the corner of the bunkhouse where his friends waited.

A little later as Kendo stood on the porch Darcy Pitt eased up beside him. The old plainsman wore moccasins and his movements were so stealthy as to be undetectable. If not for the smell of the black tobacco he burned in his corncob pipe, Kendo would not have even known that he was being approached.

'That was a mistake,' Darcy said in a near-whisper. He nodded toward the bunkhouse. 'Those three were born to trouble: Bo, Rex and Weeks.'

'You're probably right,' Kendo agreed. 'What other choice was there? Pierce doesn't want his boys along. That leaves Rush – and you know his leg is bad – young Dooley and Grant who is half blind these days if you ask me. And Cooky.'

'I guess you're right,' Darcy was forced to agree. He looked again to the bunkhouse. 'Maybe it's better to have them where we can keep a close eye on them anyway.'

'You expect trouble?' Kendo asked.

'Don't you?' Darcy replied. 'I was doin' some figuring in my head. You know what fifty prime horses are worth out here?'

'Yes,' Kendo said. He did exactly. He knew the price Frank Pierce had asked of Drew Link: $4,000. And Pierce was doing Link a favor. A few of their very good horses could have been sold for a hundred apiece, maybe more.

'A bunch of hold-up men could make more taking the herd than they'd likely get from a stage stick-up,' Darcy Pitt said, knocking the dottle out of his pipe by tapping it on his bootheel. He nodded toward the barracks. 'And the rumor I hear . . . those three have had some experience in that line of work.'

'It would take more than three men to grab the herd,' Kendo said.

'Maybe there are more,' Darcy said quietly. 'Have you thought of that?' Then he nodded, put his pipe in his pocket and wished Kendo goodnight.

Morning held bright and clear, with only a few mammoth white clouds drifting peacefully past. A light breeze shuffled the long grass. Most of the crew was already out gathering the horses. Kendo had given his instructions to Cooky who was to pack provisions for the drive. These would be carried by the ranch's ten-year old gray mare. It was hoped she would follow the herd willingly so that no one would have to be assigned to take charge of her.

Wandering toward the corral, Kendo looked over the few horses that had already been penned. He took a minute to remind Billy Collier to make sure none of them appeared lame or ill and that there was no mare heavily in foal among them. He had already told the ranch hands that, but sometimes men needed reminding. Knowing that they had only this one job to complete on this morning, a few of them might have gotten eager to finish the round-up and laze the rest of the day away.

That done, Kendo checked the stock of ammunition, hoping that they would have no cause to burn all of it and then walked across the sun-bright yard for a last meeting with Frank Pierce. The old man looked no better. Still frail, his face was papery. His white hair was spread unevenly across his pink scalp. He shifted uncomfortably from time to time in his bed as they spoke. His hip was obviously causing him considerable pain. Kendo pulled up a wooden chair and sat near the old man's bed. Pierce enquired about the weather, asked what Kendo's plans were and was briefly answered.

Pierce closed his eyes for a moment and said through dry lips, 'You know, Kendo, I'll be wrecked if this drive doesn't get through. I'll have lost my horses. The cattle are due to be delivered starting next month. If I can't pay for them with the proceeds from this sale . . . well, I'll be left with a lot of grass and little else to show for my twenty years on this range.'

'I realize that, sir,' Kendo said, handing the old man a glass of water from which he sipped.

'It's as if I've handed you my wallet to hold for me, Kendo. I trust you that much, but I also know that much can go wrong.'

'Don't worry, Mr Pierce. I'll handle it.'

Could he? Kendo wondered, as he stepped outside again to watch Aaron Collier hieing three new horses into the pen. What if he did fail? The old man had gambled all on this drive. And it was an uncertain proposition.

He walked over to the horse pen to watch the Collier brothers at their work. If not for the two or three years' difference in their ages, they might have passed for twins – both freckled with reddish hair sawn off at the shoulders, both with slightly upturned noses and guileless eyes. Aaron, the older brother, chided Billy over something and both men laughed. Kendo walked on without stopping to speak to them.

Into the yard now rode Big Bo Chandler and Rex McColl, pushing but two ponies – a blue roan and a leggy sorrel before them. They seemed to be in no hurry, or perhaps they were leaving the bulk of the labor to the other hands. Bo Chandler muttered something to McColl and the man with the narrow mustache shifted his scornful eyes toward Kendo and muttered something back. As they passed, Kendo wished again that he did not have to take these two and their pal, Charlie Weeks, along on the drive, but there had really been no choice in the matter.

Darcy Pitt and Hatha came into the yard now, driving four horses and the scout lifted a hand in greeting. The old plainsman wore his long, graying hair tied back into a tail with a bit of leather thong. Hatha, expressionless as usual, glanced at Kendo, but the Bannock did not smile, wave or lift a hand in passing. His concentration was only on his work, his little paint pony shouldering a jittery roan which suddenly balked at being fenced in, turning the animal back.

By noon, the work had been completed. Kendo tallied the ponies once again, double-checked for any infirm horses among them, and wandered back to the bunkhouse where most of the men waited dismounted.

'All right, boys,' Kendo told them. 'Get your lunch and see to your gear. Two men stand watch at the pen so we don't have any breakouts. Everyone will take a turn. Relief every two hours.'

Later, as the men sat drinking coffee – Kendo had banned whiskey on this night and on the drive – he stood up and explained things to the hands.

'This is the way we're going to work it, men. Hatha and Darcy Pitt will be outriders, north and south, watching for any trouble.'

'While we do the work,' Bo Chandler grunted.

'It'll be easier to do if you don't have to spend your time looking over your shoulder for Indians or other raiders,' Kendo said, restraining his voice. 'I'm going to take point. The rest of you on the flanks. The ponies might be a little frisky the first day or so, wishing to return to home range, but, like cattle, they'll settle in after a while and want to stick to the herd.'

'Are we expecting trouble?' Billy Collier asked.

'We have to. I haven't heard of the Cheyenne or Shoshone kicking up' – he glanced at Hatha who shook his head – 'and it's pretty well known that the Nez Perce are making their way toward Canada. But you never know. There's always a few renegades.'

'If Indians attack, there'll be a lot of shooting,' Darcy Pitt put in, around the stem of his pipe. 'Indians don't care if the herd scatters far and wide. In time the horses will find each other again. Indians just need to gather them as they come across them. If it's whites, now. . . .'

'What if it's whites?' Bo Chandler asked, with some belligerence.

Darcy answered him. 'Horse-thieves won't want the herd scattered. There's too much chance someone could catch up with them before they could gather the horses again. What they'd try to do, with as little commotion as possible, is to pick off their guardians – us – one by one.

'All right,' Kendo said. 'Meeting's over unless there are questions. No? Then double-check your weapons, turn in early, get some sleep. It's going to be a long trail.'

'How'm I supposed to get to sleep without my whiskey?' Charlie Weeks complained.

'No whiskey, Charlie. If you can't sleep, I'll let you take ceiling watch.'

Aaron Collier laughed; his brother smiled. No one else found it amusing, especially Charlie Weeks, who gave Kendo a scathing glance before stalking to his bunk where he sullenly disassembled his Colt revolver before oiling it.

Hatha had gathered up his blanket and rifle and started toward the door.

'Sleep near the herd tonight, will you, Hatha?' Kendo asked the Indian. They couldn't afford to have the horses break out and have to begin the entire process all over again in the morning. The Bannock nodded without answering and went out into the crisp night, blanket across his shoulder.

'Do you still want us to take night watch, Kendo?' Aaron Collier asked.

Kendo had been thinking that over and had come

up with a better solution. 'No, get your rest. I'll send Dooley and Ben Rush' – the youngest of the hands and the man with the gimpy leg – 'to stand the first watch. Grant can go over later.' He referred to the older ranch hand who seemed to be developing cataracts. 'Then I'll go over to the big house and ask Pierce if we can use his two sons on relief. They'll all have plenty of time to rest up after we're gone. You get some shut-eye now, Aaron, but keep your guns near at hand.

'You'd better get used to sleeping with them close by from now on.'

TWO

They shivered in the chill of the dawn. Kendo stood on the bunkhouse porch finishing his second cup of coffee watching the sky redden beyond the big oak trees in the yard. There was frost on the backs of the ponies. Aaron Collier had been sent out early to gather their second mounts in the barn and form a string of them. They would take turns leading these. Cooky, finished with making early breakfast, had already turned his attention to strapping two huge canvas sacks on to the back of the stolid gray mare that would carry their provisions toward Idaho. Darcy Pitt slipped up beside Kendo, puffing at his corncob pipe filled with that rank black tobacco.

'Ready to start?' the old plainsman asked. Standing with his pipe in his mouth, he tied his long gray hair into a tail.

'Ready?' Kendo grinned. 'I don't know, but it's time.'

With all hands mounted they began the tricky job of leading the half-wild horses out of the pen, trying to keep them grouped and calm at once. The first horse out, a wild-eyed buckskin tried to break loose and head back toward the long grass he was used to. Cursing, Kendo and Darcy caught up with it, pinching it between their own two horses. A herding animal's instinct is to always follow the leader. If this one got loose, there was a possibility that the entire herd would try to follow it. Kendo and Darcy got the buckskin turned back in the direction they wished to go.

Behind them in the pen, the now fully awakened horses reared up, kicked out and whinnied with excitement or unease. Dust rose from beneath the many hoofs; a big palomino reared up and came down again, narrowly missing Aaron Collier's head with a flailing front hoof. Great muscles flexed and the horses shook their heads as if in refusal. They were eased out of the corral singly or in pairs. It would not do to open the floodgates to all of that horseflesh. None of them had ever been driven off home range before, and they would find it unsettling, perhaps angering. The second day or the one after would find them settled to the trail, but for now they were confused and resentful.

Darcy Pitt had eased the buckskin forward slowly, westward, away from the ranch. Singly and in pairs the others fell in behind. Bo Chandler and Billy Collier flanked them as they emerged from the pen to prevent another breakout. Behind them, Rex McColl and Charlie Weeks prodded those horses that proved reluctant to leave the pen and follow along.

Darcy continued to ease the buckskin horse and its followers ahead until all of the horses had emerged from the corral and, convinced by the riders on their flanks that it was best to proceed forward, fell in behind. Cautiously, then, at Kendo's signal, Darcy began walking his own blue roan on at a reasonable speed and, glancing back frequently, led the ponies down through the trees and toward the creek bottom beyond.

Kendo closed the corral gate from horseback and started after the herd, only once glancing back to see Frank Pierce standing on the front porch of his house, supported by his sons, watching after them. Kendo rode on, all of the old man's hopes for his future and that of his sons, riding with him.

Crossing the shallow creek, they emerged on to the long, featureless plains, the horses stringing out nicely. Hatha had already ridden off to the north. Kendo spurred his big gray horse forward to the point to relieve the other outrider of his duties. He doubted they would run into any trouble this close to the home ranch, but you never knew.

'Well,' Darcy said, when Kendo caught up with him at the point, 'it's a start.'

'It's a start,' Kendo agreed. 'We'll take them just far enough to make them tired today. We should be able to make Pocono Springs easily. Tonight, we'll take turns riding watch. Hopefully they'll be content to graze and sleep, but it seems that buckskin still has it in mind that returning to the home range is a good idea.'

'It'll work, Kendo,' Darcy Pitt said.

'It has to,' Kendo answered grimily.

Without another word, Darcy turned his horse southward and rode out to assume his outrider's duty – watching for any sign of trouble.

They made it almost a mile before trouble started.

At the sound of the first shot, the startled horses did not stampede, but they became agitated. Some halted in their tracks, others tried to bolt forward, a few broke from the flanks. All of the hands – Chandler, McColl, Charlie Weeks and Aaron Collier worked like the the devil, spurring their saddle mounts to hold the bunch. The lead buckskin held his ground, though his eyes were wild. Cursing, Kendo left the point to Rex McColl who had drawn his Colt, suspecting trouble, and rode toward the rear of the herd. Then there was a second shot and the horses reacted much as before if not so violently. What damned fool. . . ?

Then Kendo saw Billy Collier's little sorrel horse standing, reins dangling, and ten feet away Billy Collier sitting on the ground, pistol in his hand. Kendo was ready to give the likeable kid hell, but as he dismounted he saw the trouble. Three feet from Billy lay a forearm-thick six foot long rattlesnake, its head blown off. Billy looked up with anxious eyes. There was pain in them as well, deep pain.

'Broke my arm. I'm sorry, Kendo,' he said, holstering his pistol, cradling his left arm in his right hand. 'My pony saw the rattler and jumped. Threw me. I damned near landed on the snake. Missed him with my first shot.'

He was grimacing with pain. Now his brother had ridden up to join them. Kendo kicked the snake aside and crouched down beside Billy. 'Are you sure it's broken?' he asked.

'Afraid so. I'm a lot of help, ain't I?'

'Want me to take him back to the ranch, Kendo?' Aaron Chandler asked, walking up beside him.

'No,' Billy said vehemently. 'I'm already leaving Kendo a man short. You stick with the herd, Aaron. I'll get myself home.'

They fashioned a rough sling out of Billy's kerchief and helped him mount his pony. Hunched over the animal's neck in pain, he heeled the sorrel and started back toward the home ranch.

'Damn all,' Kendo muttered.

He turned to see Bo Chandler sitting on his black horse, his dark eyes expressing nothing, but Kendo saw, or imagined he saw, the corner of his mouth twitch in a half-smile. Maybe, Kendo thought, Big Bo was mentally counting heads and had decided that the odds in his favor had just grown a little.

Kendo had nothing on which to base his suspicions. He was not one to trust to instincts entirely; too often some notion of his had been proved wrong. It was a little more than a feeling, however. Something in the eyes of those three – Bo Chandler, McColl and Charlie Weeks – gleamed with secret knowledge. And a man's eyes can be read. Too, there was that bunkhouse gossip that the three had stuck up a stage or two on their backtrail. True or not, it was disquieting. The three were skilled horsemen, but their manner was not that of your ordinary ranch hand.

Shaking off his unfounded suspicions for the moment, Kendo returned to the point to relieve McColl who gave him one of his scornful glances and pulled away toward the flank of the herd. Starting on, they let the grass, now shorter and growing yellow the farther they rode front the river, pass beneath the horses' hoofs without conversation. With luck they would reach Pocono Springs by sundown and the horses, trail-weary, watered and left to graze, would settle in peacefully for the night. Only one thing began to cause Kendo worry. The clouds in the northern sky had begun to thicken and grow darker. The wind had stiffened. The last thing they needed was a rainstorm. Lightning could stampede the herd and gathering them again in a downpour would prove almost impossible. The animals would scatter everywhere, some possibly still trying to return to home range.

For now, however, the storm held back and they gathered the herd at noon to hold it in place while the men ate in shifts. Food and cooking utensils were retrieved from the packs on the old gray mare's back. Thankfully the animal had proven to be no trouble at all. She needed no lead to follow along with the herd, though at a slightly slower pace than the younger horses. Aaron Collier ate rapidly and was dispatched to relieve Darcy Pitt so that the outrider could have his meal.

By the time Darcy Pitt rode in on his piebald, Kendo had finished his own meal. Walking to where Darcy had swung down and was now loosening his saddle cinches, Kendo asked, 'See anything out there, Darcy?'

'Nothing but horizon. What about Hatha?'

'He hasn't ridden in. Probably waiting for relief. I'll go out and let him come in and grab a bite.'

Bo Chandler had already begun packing some of the supplies again. From horseback, Kendo told him. 'Leave enough out for Hatha to have a meal.'

'The Indian?' Chandler snorted. 'He's probably out there digging up roots for his supper.'

Rex McColl thought that was funny. No one else cracked a smile. Hatha was respected and well liked despite his solitary ways. Kendo turned his gray's head away without replying and started out to the northern flank to relieve Hatha.

It should not have been difficult since Hatha knew where the horse herd was located and his job was to stay to the north of it, but Kendo could not find the Bannock. He cast to the east and west, keeping his eyes on the far horizon and occasionally eyeing any stand of brush carefully, remembering what had happened to Billy Collier. Hatha was a superb horseman, but any man can be thrown. He hated to think of Hatha lying in a gully with a broken leg with no chance of anyone hearing his calls for help.

Kendo glanced back and saw that the horses were again on the move toward Pocono Springs. Well, he thought, they couldn't have waited forever and it was now well over an hour since he had started out to look for Hatha.

The storm continued to gather and the clouds to bulk larger against the sky. Distantly he heard the low grumbling of thunder. With more urgency he continued his search for the missing outrider. With other Indians, with some other whites, he might have considered that Hatha had decided that he no longer cared for the job and had just lit out for home. But Hatha was intensely loyal to Frank Pierce and had never been known to shirk any responsibility.

There was no trace of the man! Kendo began playing scout, searching for tracks in the sandy soil. Again he had no luck. What now? He was beginning to worry. Even if he hadn't seen Hatha, the Bannock should have been traveling west now, roughly parallel to the herd, and the Bannock would certainly have seen Kendo, since his job as outrider was to spot any riders lurking near the herd.

He was beginning to feel certain that something had happened to him. The feeling knotted his stomach and caused him to push the gray horse on with more urgency. But in what direction should he search? Had Hatha continued westward; had something caused him to turn back on the trail, perhaps having spotted something, someone that needed inspection? Kendo's search seemed suddenly futile despite his fears.

He did all that he could think of doing and turned his pony westward, replacing the missing Hatha as outrider.

The herd was now left to Aaron Collier, Rex McColl, Bo Chandler and Charlie Weeks. It was a miserable decision that Kendo was forced to make, but he could think of no other at the moment. It would have to do at least until night camp at Pocono when someone would be sent out to look for *him.*

Kendo rode on gloomily. The wind was still increasing and the bulking clouds drew nearer. If the storm reached them there would be no need for an outrider. Visibility would be so limited that an approaching army could not be seen or heard above the rain and roar it would carry. Too, if the storm hit, every man they had would be needed to keep the herd gathered. They would be spooked by thunder and lightning, hard to contain.

Regretfully Kendo turned his horse's head southward.

And came upon Hatha.

The Bannock was sprawled against the earth at the bottom of a shallow arroyo. His blanket lay near him, but there was no sign of the paint pony.

Dismounting, Kendo slid down the bank of the gully and went to the Indian. Hatha did not move. He was either badly hurt, or. . . .

Had his horse been spooked by something and thrown him? Kendo crouched beside the motionless Bannock and rolled him over. Hatha's black eyes had no light in them. Dead. Kendo swallowed a curse and felt Hatha's body to see if his neck had been broken in a fall. It had not.

Now that he had been rolled on to his back the bullet hole through the front of his yellow shirt was obvious. Kendo rose cautiously and searched the darkening land with his eyes. He kept his hand on his revolver as he inched back up the slope to where his horse stood waiting. Nothing moved across the plains, nothing spoke but the rumbling thunder.

There was no time to bury Hatha and nothing to do the job with. Silently apologizing to the faithful Indian, he reached for his pony's reins and felt the sudden burning impact of a bullet as it grooved its way across his shoulder. Kendo dropped to the ground, but there was no shelter from the sniper's shots. He had lost his horse's reins. Now he rose in a crouch to try to snatch them up again. He needed to ride, to get away from here before he and Hatha shared a common unmarked grave.

The second bullet, fired from a great distance,

caught Kendo in the back, high up beneath the wing bone on the right side and he went down again, this time on his face. His pony danced away, and this time Kendo did not try to collect the animal, This time he could not. He lay face down, motionless as unheard thunder shook the earth, unseen lightning struck close at hand and unfelt cold rain drove down.

THREE

It was full dark when Kendo's eyes opened. He lay still, staring at a stormy night where rain sheeted down, where the only light was the occasional flickering of bone-white lightning. It was cold, very cold. It took him a moment to mentally review what had happened to him, how he had come to this, but as his mind cleared he knew that he was now in a desperate situation. Exposed to the elements, cut off from his men, wounded to an unknown extent, without shelter or warm clothing.

He needed to find his horse. Failing that, he needed to try to make Pocono Springs afoot. How far was that? Five miles, ten? He had lost track. First he had to rise, if that was possible. Thunder boomed again as he tried to get to his feet in the normal way. The pain in his back would not allow it and he sagged back to the earth which was now sodden and cold. With his face half-buried in the mud he tried again. The furrow across his shoulder burned even in the chill of night, but that was not hampering him. Each movement of his right arm, however, was impeded by the pain it engendered. There was a bullet wedged in his back, interfering with the mechanics of his body.

There had to be a way. Kendo rolled on to his back, again triggering blinding pain. Bracing his left arm, he tucked his left leg under him, rolled to his knee and finally managed to stand erect – or as near to erect as he could hope for. The pain caused him to half-double over. Rain streamed down, washing his hair into his face, obscuring all. He stood breathing raggedly, forcing his foggy mind to think.

South. He had to head south and west to find Pocono Springs where the herd was to be halted on this night. All right – the storm had arisen in the north. The wind, therefore was to be his rough compass. He turned his back to the gusting wind and began walking. Even with the fierce pain his wound was causing, he was grateful that the sniper had not tagged his leg. He was able to walk, to pursue, even if he was afoot. He had all night to find the herd. So long as he kept walking, he had a chance.

His pony was long gone. He hoped it had returned

to the herd. If it had gone back riderless, someone would have been sent out to look for him, although they could not see him any more than he would have been able to see a passing horsemen only a few yards away from him through the teeth of the storm. Help was a flimsy hope. He would have to save himself.

Kendo plodded on hopefully, the wind and rain at his back. The rain was falling too hard to be absorbed by the soil and the earth was a long bog, inches thick in red mud. Twice he stepped into pools of cold water that reached above his boot tops and seeped in, numbing his feet. Thunder roared constantly and the cold northern wind buffeted his back. Going down over an unseen rock, he landed roughly on his right shoulder and the shock of pain kept him inert against the earth for long minutes until he pried himself up and started on once more through the darkness, fiery pain gnawing at his back.

How far to Pocono Springs? Not in miles, not in hours, but in steps? How many more jolting stiff-legged steps would he have to take before he could hope to reach help? A million, he suspected, no more.

The strange ozone in the air and the bitter cold made it difficult to take in a deep breath. Breathing through his clamped teeth he fought his way forward. Sometime, hours, days, years later the silver moon broke briefly through a ragged cleft in the dark clouds and by its pale glow he saw – or thought he saw, a stand of willow trees to the south, slightly behind him. This could be Pocono Springs. Had to be! He had overshot it, and only by the small grace of the unexpected glimmer of the briefly appearing moon had he managed to spot the trees at all. Had he kept on going as he was he would have ended up far out on the empty plains, walking until he fell from exhaustion, falling to lie until he was frozen to death.

With new determination, he started toward the stand of trees. Even if it was not Pocono, the trees offered some sort of shelter, some protection from the gale winds. He could not find the trees! He searched one way and the other, wasting his time, using up his limited supply of remaining strength in a futile search. Why not lie down? Why not just give it all up? His mind, numbed by the cold, could not come up with a good reason to keep on through the driving rain.

A horse whickered.

And not far away. Kendo stood stock still, waiting prayerfully. There was a horse nearby. Somewhere. He heard it again and started in that direction. Or in the direction the wind-bent sound seemed to be coming from.

Then stark and shivering against the gray skies, he saw the even darker shadows of swaying treetops. He hurried forward like a madman, stumbling and staggering toward the willow trees. It was Pocono Springs, had to be. He had caught up with them after all. He eased his way through the tightly bunched trees and their tangled shadows. Moving more by touch than sight, his hands stretched out like a sleepwalker's, feeling for the trunks of the shaggy willows. He called out, tried it again, but received no response. But then he doubted that someone more than twenty feet away could have heard his voice above the howling wash of the storm.

He nearly walked into the horse. He felt its body heat, saw the dull glimmer in its eye, and his hand touched flesh. He seized its mane with his left hand. The animal was not going to elude him. By the feeble light he saw first that its hide appeared gunmetal steel, dark gray with the wash of the rain, and he believed that to his incredible luck he had managed to find his own mount again. It was not his horse.

It was the old gray mare, the party's pack horse.

Then, at least, the others were nearby. No campfire burned, but he reflected, none would have stayed lit in these conditions. He called again, leading the docile mare forward by its mane. The trees fell away and he found himself in a clearing where a fire ring had been built. The canvas sacks the mare had been carrying were there, empty and rain-soaked, flat against the ground. Kendo called again, but he received no answer.

They were gone.

The riders, the herd, everyone.

That could not be, should not be. A dim uneasiness began to creep into his mind. This gradually became certainty. The herd had been stolen. Why had the old mare been left behind? – simple: the creature was incredibly slow. They had spilt up the provisions and left the gray mare behind. That seemed to mean that they intended now to move far and fast.

The only men he had trusted were Aaron Collier and, of course, Darcy Pitt. What had been done to them? Maybe they had been involved as well. Kendo shook that unworthy suspicion away. Both were loyal to the brand, to Frank Pierce.

Surely it would take more than three men to drive the herd ahead. But he remembered mentioning this to Darcy Pitt before the drive had even begun, and Darcy's response: 'Maybe there are more. Have you ever thought of that?'

Now what? Was he to pursue a band of armed men into the teeth of the storm on this dark night, knowing he would never be able to find their tracks in this weather with the ground a sloppy mess. He had no idea which direction they had chosen. He knew they were hours ahead of him and there was no way at all he was going to be able to pursue them or hope to have any success even if he could, miraculously, catch up with the herd.

He had failed once again.

Frank Pierce's herd was gone, the profit he hoped to make from its sale, the money he needed to pay for the purchase of his cattle. The man would be broken. The price men always paid when they left their affairs in Kendo's hands.

Just ask Carly Barrett.

The pain throbbing in Kendo's back reminded him that there were other reasons to keep moving. If he did not get that bullet removed from his back, and soon, he would die from it or the crippling bursts of pain which seemed to grow more intense with each repetition.

It took three agonizing attempts, but finally he managed to hoist himself on to the gray mare's back and heel it into motion, headed for. . . .

Carly Barrett had found Kendo just as he finished tamping in the last fence post on the southern line of the Corn Creek Ranch. From horseback, Carly gestured to him. Putting his shovel aside, Kendo, sweating, bare-chested in the heat of the August sun, walked to the ranch-owner's horse, mopping his face with his red kerchief.

Carly was an amiable, gray-haired man of middle years with an untrimmed yellow-gray mustache. He sat his pinto pony lazily.

'Yes, Mr Barrett?' Kendo said, squinting up into the brilliant sunlight.

'Had enough posthole digging for today?'

'I'm about through.'

'Good,' Barrett said, with a pleasant, yellow-toothed smile. He turned his head to spit out a stream of tobacco juice, cuffed his lips and said, 'Rinse off and come over to the big house. I need to talk to you about something.'

Washing up a little, Kendo put on a clean white shirt and walked across the yard through the shade of the dusty elm trees toward the porch of the big, green trimmed white house. Barrett was waiting for him in his cool, scantily furnished office. A small leather case sat on the otherwise empty desk. Barrett looked up, nodded Kendo into a chair and told him, 'I need you to ride into Tortuga for me.'

'All right,' Kendo agreed. He did not ask the reason. Barrett nudged the leather case toward him with one stubby finger.

'This has to get to the bank today, Kendo. As you

know I have to meet my wife and daughter, Lil, in Descanso. I don't have the time to do both. What is in the case represents the profit from the last cattle sale. I need it to cover my mortgage, the payment on the loan I drew from the bank last summer when the drought hit us so hard. It has to get there' – Barrett leaned both forearms on the desk – 'today.'

'Want me to take any of the boys with me?'

'No, that would make it look too much like what it is – a cash transfer. I'm not a hundred per cent sure I trust all of the boys working for me, these days anyway. Take it yourself. Hand it personally to McGraw at the bank and get a signed receipt.'

'All right,' Kendo agreed, rising from the chair. Barrett watched him for a long minute.

'I can't tell you how important this is, Kendo. Don't let me down.'

'I won't,' Kendo had promised. But he did.

Riding out shortly after noon, the leather pouch stuffed into his saddle-bags, Kendo rode through the glare of sunlight into the hills separating the Corn Creek range from the town of Tortuga beyond.

He entered the cut where the road had been carved through the hills and had just crested out when two men appeared in the road ahead of him. Frowning, Kendo drew up his pony. He glanced behind him to see another man, masked, shotgun in his hands.

Kendo started to draw his pistol but was warned sharply by one of the masked men, 'Don't! That shotgun will cut you in half, mister.'

One of the two men in front of him approached the horse, blue bandanna across his face. He reached up, snatched Kendo's Colt from his holster and tucked it behind his belt.

'Swing down, partner, or we'll shoot you off that pony's back.'

'What do you want?' Kendo asked, as his boots touched down, but there was no need to ask. They knew. The leather pouch was retrieved from the saddle-bags and held up triumphantly. Kendo could not fight back. He attempted at least to identify the men. He had no luck at that either. Perhaps if he had seen their horses . . . but these were well-concealed. He did notice that the man with the shotgun had his middle finger on the triggers. The first finger of his right hand was missing.

For the rest of it – their hats were tugged low, they wore slickers to conceal their clothing and bandannas to hide their faces.

'You won't get anything out of this,' Kendo said in a dry voice. 'They'll track you down.'

One of them laughed and said, 'They'd better be ready to ride long and hard then.'

'And so had you,' the man with the shotgun warned Kendo.

'I don't take your meaning.'

'Do you think that anyone is going to believe you when you tell them that you were held up? We know how to cover our tracks, friend. They'll find nothing to prove we were even here. At the least they'll lock you up and try to sweat the truth out of you. Asking you where you hid the cash. At the worst, they'll send you off to prison. Either way, you won't have a job any more, will you? No, partner, the safest thing for you to do is just ride out of this country as well.'

The three disappeared into the roadside brush and after a while Kendo heard horses plodding away. His first instinct was to go after them – and do what? Unarmed against three highwaymen he had no chance of accomplishing a thing.

His second notion was to ride back to the ranch and wait for Barrett's return, to swallow humiliation and own up to losing the money, which would likely be chalked up to his carelessness. No matter – as the outlaw had said, he would certainly be fired after Barrett scalded him with his tongue. He would find himself packing up his gear as unpitying eyes in the bunkhouse, suspicious eyes, watched. No one on the Corn Creek would ever again trust him, nor be sure whether or not Kendo had actually stolen the money himself.

In the end, with a sense of shame and guilt, he took the outlaw's advice and simply skulked away from further disgrace, riding northward toward a land where he was not known as a thief and a coward.

It was probably the worst mistake Kendo had ever made in his life, but he had been even younger and dumber then, unable to handle the disgrace that would surely have been attached to him.

It would not happen again! He would not allow it. He had suffered through enough miserable nights recalling the events of that day. This time he would follow the bandits; he would not rest until they were brought to justice or he, Kendo, was dead. Death before dishonor – he wondered who had first said that. Now he believed he fully understood the forgotten man who had phrased it that way. The dishonor he had carried so long had become a grinding weight on his heart.

Sudden death could be no worse.

He rode the heavy-footed gray mare on through the drive and whip of the thrashing storm. Without a saddle to cling to, he fell not once but twice that night, only to awake uncounted minutes later, sprawled against the ooze of the red mud to struggle again to his feet and clamber aboard the mare which each time remained fixed in place for him, patiently waiting for the man to finish whatever he was doing and urge her on once more.

The last time Kendo rose to stand leaning against the mare, breathing raggedly, painfully, each breath sending a surge of pain through his wounded back, he slowly realized that something had changed.

The wind had lessened, the low clouds were breaking. The rain was stuttering to a stop, and the eastern skies were beginning to flare with the light of scarlet morning.

He had made it through the night. It was a small triumph, but it seemed huge at that moment. If he had lived through the storm, the gunshots, he could do anything.

If only he could manage to drag himself once more on to the gray mare's back. . . .

But he could not. His hand gripped the horse's mane with all of the strength in his weary body, but the strength that remained was not enough to allow him to throw himself up and on to the animal's back. After the third try, with his back bleeding fiery pain he simply gave up – there was no choice – and he sagged to the ground to lie in the mud.

A light mist continued to fall for a while, but Kendo hardly felt it on his face. He stared upward into the sunrise sky, watching it color. There was some deep purple, but for the most part it was as red as fire beyond the scattering clouds. He watched the colors shift as if he were watching a kaleidoscope, a show put on for his benefit alone.

Across the crimson sky small black clouds danced and twisted like leggy young colts gamboling across the sky racing with the wind, and shadowy, racing mustangs pursued by prairie wolves. There were dark, uncertain faces there as well: men he had seen but never known; men he had known but never seen. Women longed for and neither seen nor known.

It was an Arctic cold that settled slowly over him, but after a while he no longer shivered. After a while he no longer felt the chill of morning, the damp of it. He still wanted to rise, but his body refused him.

Kendo knew that if he could just get to his feet, he could make it. Penance could be offered and retribution gained. If only he could clamber to his feet and reach what lay ahead, beyond the crimson skies.

He closed his eyes, stretched an arm skyward and entered the dark door of dreamless sleep.

FOUR

The blurred colors of the sunrise swam before his eyes. Or behind them – Kendo could not be sure. He was feverish and racked with pain. The gray mare still stood there, studying him dumbly. Confused, abandoned, it by now must have been terrifically hungry and nearly as cold as Kendo himself. Still the loyal creature stood by him.

If only he could rise . . . but he could not. Lifting himself on to one elbow sent shattering pain through his body and he slumped back, breathing as if that minor exertion was a day's labor.

He knew that he would never rise again, not on his own. He heard something then, or thought he did. He wiped the mud from his eyes and then reached carefully, slowly toward his holstered Colt.

He saw them then. Silhouetted figures, black

against the crimson skies and he nearly drew his gun before one of them spoke.

'What happened to you, cowboy?'

It was a woman's voice. There were two of them he now saw. They had arrived on a buckboard, the wheels of the machine making no sound across the muddy earth. As his eyes focused he saw that one of them, in a long blue dress and blue hat remained on the bench seat of the wagon while the other, in men's clothes had hopped down to approach him.

'Where are you from, cowboy?' the younger, tomboyish girl asked.

'Corn Creek,' Kendo said dully.

'Never heard of it. It must be a ways off.'

'Long way. . . .'

'Where'd they get you?'

'My back. I can't get up,' Kendo replied thickly.

'We'll send somebody back, Lonnie,' the woman on the buckboard said.

'No. We can't leave him lying out here, Carla! He won't make it.'

Kendo saw now that both women were blonde. The older one, the girl on the buckboard had her hair pinned and curled, tightly coifed. The younger, the one crouched over him wore her hair in a single long pigtail. She looked up to her sister.

'Show a little mercy. So it's inconvenient! We can't

leave anyone out here. It could be one of us needing help some day.'

'Do what you want then,' the woman named Carla said, with a hint of disgust.

'We've got to get him into Ambrose. They have a doctor there now.'

'That's ten miles out of our way.'

'It is,' Lonnie agreed. She rose now, wiping her hands on her blue jeans. 'Can't we afford that much time to save a man's life?'

'I suppose so,' Carla answered without pleasure. 'Get him up into the bed, then.'

'You'll have to help me,' Lonnie said. She had her hands on her hips. Her voice had grown sharp.

With distaste Carla looked down at the thick mud, glanced at her prettily shined boots and with the heaviest of sighs said, 'All right then! But if my new boots are ruined. . . .'

'I'll buy you another pair.'

'These came all the way from Denver, remember?'

'Carla!' the younger girl said with exasperation.

'Oh, all right. I said I'd do it, didn't I?'

As if being forced to wade into a cesspool, Carla hoisted her skirts and descended from the buckboard. The two women got on either side of Kendo and strained to lift him to his feet. Raging pain returned, shooting through his back, Kendo gritted his teeth, trying to fight back the wave of blackness threatening to send him again into unconsciousness. The crimson in the dawn sky had begun to fade to pink. Clear light lit the far mountain peaks.

With a thump he landed on his back in the bed of the buckboard where various packages lay. Carla, still grumbling, clambered back up on to the spring seat of the buckboard, lamenting her soiled shoes and the muddy hem of her blue skirt. Lonnie caught up the reins of the gray mare and tethered it on behind. With a fleeting, sad sort of smile, she returned to the buckboard's seat, gathered up the reins and started the two-horse team onward.

The sun was hot and yellow in Kendo's eyes before they reached the town they had called Ambrose. Looking up and out, Kendo watched a row of false-fronted buildings pass by, heard someone call out to the buckboard, saw three riders tip their hats to the women, murmuring between themselves after they passed. One man laughed.

The wagon jolted and slid down the muddy, rutted main street and jerked to a stop beside a white-washed single-story building.

'I'll see if the doctor is here,' Lonnie said, putting on the brake, wrapping the reins around it. She leaped down agilely and went away.

'You're ruining my plans for this morning,' Carla said, glancing back at Kendo.

'Sorry,' he muttered. Carla and Lonnie looked much alike, but Carla's blue eyes were harder, her face squarer, her mouth which was full, drawn tightly. Maybe she was beautiful when she was in a gay mood, but just now her demeanor was that of an angry schoolteacher after some student has spilled his ink.

'Half an hour,' he heard Lonnie say, as she returned. 'He's over at the Tim Tam. The bartender had his hand broken trying to break up a fight last night.'

'Well, then?' Carla asked.

'Well, then, we get the patient here inside. Doctor Hollister's son will be right out to help.'

'Can't stand that little brat,' Carla said.

Her sister did not respond. Instead she seated herself on the tailgate and told Kendo, 'It'll be all right. Hollister's a good doctor.' Kendo only managed to smile his gratitude. His throat felt constricted. He couldn't remember the last time he had taken a drink of water. He felt parched, dehydrated and weak as a kitten. He had nearly passed out again by the time the doctor's son – a large-shouldered boy of fourteen or so came out to the wagon.

'What happened to him?' the kid asked.

'Shot in the back along the trail,' Lonnie answered.

'Seems to be a lot of that going on these days. OK. Let me go back in and grab a stretcher.'

The stretcher was shoved up into the wagon bed beside Kendo and with a lot of maneuvering they managed to get him on to the contraption. They were trying to be gentle about it, but Kendo's back had gotten to the point where the slightest movement was agonizing.

Kendo supposed he blacked out again for a few minutes. When he next opened his eyes he was lying in bed in a cubbyhole of a room, a lantern burning on a bedside table. There was a clean sheet over him and, blinking his eyes, he realized that someone had taken the time to wash his mud-caked face.

The kid was sitting in the corner, chewing on a sourdough roll. Noticing that Kendo was awake, he asked, 'Who got you?' with boyish curiosity.

'Don't know. Never saw 'em.'

'That's the way it's been happening around here lately,' the boy said. 'Take it easy, mister. My father won't be long in coming. He's a lot of experience removing bullets.' The kid added, 'Lucky for you the Link girls found you and brought you in.'

The Link girls? Like in Drew Link, the man for whom the stolen horses were destined? Kendo enquired.

'Sure. Drew Link, owner of the DL Ranch. They're his daughters. Lonnie is all right; as for Carla. . . .' his voice trailed off as the front door opened and closed again and bootsteps approached across the wooden floor. 'That's Dad,' the kid said, rising. 'Don't worry about a thing, There's nothing he don't know about gunshot wounds. Not being in practise in this town.'

Kendo remembered that the doctor's hands had been soft and sure, that the chloroform had lulled him into a cloudy sleep without sound or sight. That when he first awoke he had a terrific headache, the after-effect of the anesthesia. He knew that his back was painful if he moved, that he was wound around with a bandage. That he lay in the small room off the doctor's office.

That was all he could remember at first, and all that he cared to remember. Later as he lay propped up in the bed, he began to recall it all: Frank Pierce, the trail drive. Hatha murdered, himself ambushed.

Where was the herd now? What had happened to Aaron Collier and to Darcy Pitt? Would the outlaws have killed them too? Perhaps not, knowing that there was no way three men could handle a herd that size on their own.

Perhaps he was doing Bo Chandler, McColl and Charlie Weeks an injustice. It could be that this was none of their doing, although he did not believe that in his innermost convictions. It could be . . . there was perspiration on his forehead. His feet were cold. His back ached and his head throbbed. He gave up trying to figure it out for the moment, but sleep would not come and so he lay staring at the blank wooden wall until the younger Hollister – hadn't his father called him Frank? – came in with a bowl of broth. Beyond him sunlight glittered brightly through the front window of the doctor's office.

'Feel like eating?' the kid asked with a grin.

'Not much, but I suppose I'd better. . . . Frank, is it?'

'That's me,' the eager kid answered, drawing up a wooden chair to sit beside Kendo. 'Want me to spoon it to you, or can you handle it yourself?'

'I'll give it a try,' Kendo replied.

'You're weak now, but you'll come back strong. Dad plucked this out of you.' Frank Hollister showed Kendo a misshapen .44 caliber bullet. 'Want it for a souvenir?'

'No, you keep it.'

'I'd have quite a collection if I kept all the ones Father has dug out around here,' Frank said, still smiling. He tucked the spent lead into a vest pocket and watched as Kendo awkwardly spoon-fed himself.

Frank Hollister wore his smile for a few minutes

more, then, as Kendo's bowl was emptied, his brow began to furrow with concern. The amusement had vanished from his eyes. Kendo handed the boy the bowl and asked, 'What's the matter, Frank?'

'I usually do this for my father. . . .' he faltered. 'But I don't like it any more than he does.'

'What is it?' Kendo asked. He already had an inkling.

'After surgery's been done,' Frank said, 'and a reasonable time has passed . . . you can't stay here. You understand, don't you? We need this room for the next banged-up man that happens along.'

'I understand, yes,' Kendo said quietly.

'It's not a personal thing,' Frank Hollister said in a rush of words, 'it's just policy. We have to have this room available. You're going to have to find another place.'

'I see.' In Ambrose where he knew no one. He had no money for a hotel room. There had been no need to carry cash along the trail. 'Have you any suggestions?'

'It depends . . . you're dead broke?'

'I've three dollars I can give your father. Or I did. After that, yes, I am totally broke.'

'I wish I could. . . .' The kid looked miserable. 'But it's Friday night. If some of the boys start cutting up. . . .'

'I understand, Frank,' Kendo assured the boy. 'I've camped out half my life. If I can get to my horse. . . .' He tried to rise, found himself incapable of doing so.

'You don't have to go this minute!' Frank reassured him. 'I just wanted to let you know how things were. This isn't a hospital, is all I meant.'

'I understand you,' Kendo answered. 'If I can only get a few more hours' sleep, I'll be all right.'

He was lying and Frank knew it, nevertheless the kid accepted the lie, smiled weakly and went out with bowl and spoon, closing the door to the tiny room behind him. Kendo, having no other escape, fell off again to a slightly more troubled sleep.

The bootsteps beyond the door woke him a few hours later. When the door opened he saw the sundown was coloring the skies beyond the office window. Silhouetted in the doorway was a vaguely familiar person. When she turned to profile to speak to someone he could not see, he saw that it was unmistakably a woman who entered his room. When the lantern was lit he recognized Lonnie Link.

She sat down beside the bed, folding her hands together. Lantern light flickered on the walls and burnished her yellow hair, now worn drawn loosely back, tied with a pale-blue ribbon.

'How are you feeling?' Lonnie asked.

'I'm all right.'

'You look it!' she said.

'Not all right, then. I *will* be all right,' Kendo told her.

'Sure you will,' Lonnie said. Her smile was faint, her eyes inquisitive. 'But not for a few days. I came to take you over to the ranch.'

'The ranch?' Kendo couldn't follow her at first. His mind was still fuzzy.

'The DL,' Lonnie said. 'We can at least give you a cot in the bunkhouse until you're well enough to ride again.'

'Why would you. . . ?'

'Why would I help a dog in the street that's been hit by a wagon?' Lonnie said. 'Because we all need help sometimes. Right now, it's you who needs some.'

'I couldn't—'

'You can't do anything else, not on your own,' Lonnie said insistently, and she rose to go. 'Whenever you can, try to get yourself dressed. Want me to send Frank in to help you out?'

Kendo nodded and said unhappily. 'It might be necessary.'

Lonnie walked to the door, opened it, stood for a moment uncertainly, her hand on the brass doorknob, then went on through. The sky was growing dark.

Damn all! Kendo thought. Evicted from the surgery, he did desperately need a place to recuperate, but the DL Ranch! He had known that sooner or later he would have to face Drew Link, but not so soon. He had to tell Drew Link that the horses he meant to purchase from Frank Pierce had been lost, stolen. That Kendo had failed. That would be followed by the long ride back to the home ranch where he would have to report the same news to Pierce.

It was Corn Creek all over again. Except that this time, he vowed, he would not slink away. Someone was owed retribution, and once he was well again, Kendo vowed to deliver it personally.

The buckboard jolted on beneath the star-cluttered night sky. Kendo lay in a pile of blankets in the bed of the wagon as Lonnie guided the team homeward expertly. The first few miles rolled by without a word passing between them, but after a while Kendo wearied of the silence. He felt the girl was ignoring him, only doing some duty. Taking an injured dog back to sleep in the barn. Maybe that was all that it was to her. Nevertheless, looking up, he tried talking to her.

'Lonnie?'

'Oh,' she said, turning to look down at him. 'I

thought that you were asleep.'

'No. Is your father . . . what kind of mood is he in?'

'He's just fine,' she said with surprise. 'Why would you ask a question like that?'

'I was thinking he might not like you dragging a stranger home.'

'He knew what I was going to do, he didn't say anything against it,' Lonnie answered.

'I see. How much farther is the DL?'

'About seven miles.'

'Must get kind of lonesome all the way out here,' Kendo commented.

'I suppose so. It doesn't bother me, though, not like it does Carla. My sister is going to scream if we don't get to San Francisco soon. She's been waiting forever.'

'San Francisco?' Kendo repeated as the buckboard jolted over a rut.

'She wants to go to school there, see a real city. You're right about it being lonesome – and boring – out on the ranch, but I keep busy. Carla just sits and mopes, reading books about San Francisco, Paris and other places far away. Father finally relented. Says that Carla should at least have the chance to see the city, decide what sort of life she wants to lead, and so we're leaving sometime this month.'

'You're going too?'

'I'm not crazy to go,' Lonnie admitted, 'but Father doesn't like the idea of Carla being alone in a big city like San Francisco, so I'm going along as well.'

'Even when you don't want to?'

Lonnie's answer was firm, 'She's my sister: I'd do anything for her. Besides,' she said, her tone lightening, 'it's not going to kill me, and I can always come back to the ranch.'

Kendo was silent for a while, thinking. At length he said, 'Isn't that going to cost a lot – supporting you two in San Francisco?'

'That was one reason Father wouldn't let Carla go before. Now something's happened, some big deal came through and Father has agreed to let us go.'

Kendo asked tentatively, 'Did this all happen suddenly?'

'Very suddenly. Just in the past few days. That's why Carla was so hectic when we found you, eager to get home and not be sidetracked. You saw her – she's not mean, just eager to start on her great adventure.'

'I can understand that,' Kendo said.

Drew Link had just decided in the last day or so that he could afford to send his daughters to San Francisco. He had had some sort of big deal come through. What else had happened in the past few days?

The herd of horses that Frank Pierce was selling to

Drew Link had been stolen.

Kendo did not know Drew Link. But suppose a man was set to purchase something for $4,000 and then found a way to get that something for nothing and keep the $4,000 in his pocket? Then he could afford to send his daughters off to school in a big city like San Francisco, could he not?

Kendo did not like the way his thoughts were tending, and he was more uneasy than ever about having to meet Mr Drew Link.

FIVE

The little man with the thinning red hair was called Handy. Hatless, his tiny eyes disapproving, he approached the buckboard as Lonnie stepped down. He glanced in the bed of the wagon.

'Let's get him inside, Handy. But gently!' she remonstrated, as Handy reached for Kendo as if he were a sack of grain to be unloaded.

Handy was no born nurse, but he helped Lonnie take Kendo into a small unlighted room and lay him on a thin cot without causing any further damage. A lantern was lighted and Handy was dismissed.

'This will have to do,' Lonnie apologized. The room was no larger than the doctor's surgery had been. A picture of a girl in red tights torn from the *Police Gazette* hung on one wall. The lantern rested on a side table with one drawer. There was a small open closet and a tiny window high on the wall.

'It'll do fine,' Kendo said gratefully. 'It surely beats the open prairie.'

'Well,' Lonnie said, looking around, arms akimbo, 'it's not much. This is usually the foreman's room, but Thad is away right now. I thought you'd get more peace and quiet here than in the barracks proper. Once those men start rough-housing, well. . . .'

'It's fine,' Kendo said. 'It couldn't be better. I thank you again.'

'I'll send someone over with food for you. Right now I have to report to Father. He gets nervous if he doesn't know where Carla and I are at all times.'

'That'll make it rough for him once you've gone to San Francisco.'

'Yes, well, he's gotten used to the idea.'

Kendo didn't know what to say to that and so he said nothing. Lonnie swept out of the tiny room, leaving the door open a crack, The lantern seemed to burn with unnatural brightness. He had just closed his eyes against its glare when he heard the door open again and he looked up to see a narrow, dark girl with wide eyes creeping in softly, carrying a tray.

'I'm awake,' Kendo said.

'I see that,' the woman said with acerbity. She

placed the tray down on the bedside stand and started away.

'Is something the matter?' Kendo asked.

'No,' the dark-haired girl spat. 'Nothing at all. Don't you ever think I get tired of tending to you shot-up locos?'

With that she went out, slamming the door upon exiting. Kendo gave a little shrug, half-smiled and tried to ease himself into a position comfortable enough to attempt eating his meal. It was an hour before the hot-tempered girl came back to retrieve the empty tray. He tried to ingratiate himself.

'I'm sorry if I am interfering with your routine. . . .' he began.

'This is my routine!' she said angrily. Trying to scoop up the tray hastily, she knocked the blue ceramic cup on it to the floor and, muttering to herself, she stooped to pick it up. From her knees she said, 'I spend half my time taking care of men too stupid to keep themselves from being shot up. It is a sport in this section of Idaho, I think – shooting at each other.'

'I was only a bystander in the game,' Kendo said with a smile. 'And it was a game I didn't even understand.'

'I am sorry,' she said, her features smoothing as she rose. 'It has been a hard day.'

'It's all right. My name's Kendo,' he replied, the obvious question lingering behind his words.

'Nita,' she responded. 'Around here everyone calls me Nita.'

When Nita again returned, the open door revealed a star-cluttered sky smudged with a few ragged clouds. Kendo said nothing as she placed his supper on the table beside the bed. He reflected that he had been doing nothing but eating and sleeping. It was for the best he knew, giving his body time to heal, but already he was anxious to be up and moving, to be doing *something*.

For a time as he ate, Nita sat in the corner chair, hands clasped together between her knees in the folds of her striped skirt. Her eyes were liquid brown in the lantern light, her small mouth turned down slightly. What was it that the small, dark-haired woman had to worry about? He wanted to ask, but it was none of his business, and whatever it was, he could do nothing about it.

Not knowing what else to say, he asked her, 'Have you seen Lonnie?'

'She won't be coming back around,' Nita said with a touch of bitterness. Kendo did not respond, did not know how to. It seemed the two women did not get along. Every home, every ranch, every family had its own problems, and Kendo did not pry any further.

It didn't matter, after all. He was out of the weather, being fed. An injured stray dog brought home to mend. Why should he expect any more? Kendo wriggled around in his bed and repositioned his pillow. He slept again, more comfortably than he had in days.

While Kendo was gratefully devouring his beans and bacon, those gathered in the big house were dining more leisurely, and better. Beneath the lighted candelabrum, the table had been set with bone china decorated with tiny painted bluebells. The meal had consisted of ham, partridge, candied yams and rice pudding for desert. Drew Link was a man who valued his stomach.

The owner of the DL Ranch sat at the head of the table, his long black mustache in sharp contrast to his silver hair. His nose was aquiline, his gray eyes keen beneath heavy white eyebrows.

Lonnie wore a plain white dress, her hair sporting a red bow. Across from her, her sister wore a slinky gray silk dress and a strand of pearls. She sat near to the returned ranch foreman, Thad Connely, a man of bulk yet surprising agility. Connely was clean shaven, ruddy despite the days he spent in the sun, with large hands and deceptively quiescent dark eyes.

'Sorry about commandeering your room, Thad,'

Drew Link said, folding his linen napkin and placing it aside. 'You know how Lonnie is.'

'That's all right,' Thad Connely said, smiling at Lonnie. 'I don't mind bunking with the boys for a day or two. How bad was the man shot up?'

'A shallow burn across one shoulder, a pretty serious slug in his back,' Lonnie responded. She was still toying with her rice pudding, stirring it with a small silver spoon.

'What did you say his name was?' her father asked.

'Frank called him Kendo.'

'Frank?' Drew Link asked, his eyebrows drawing together in a frown of puzzlement.

'Doc Hollister's son,' Carla reminded him. Her eyes never left Thad Connely. He seemed to know it and accept her admiration as his due.

'Kendo?' Connely repeated. 'Is he from around here?'

'No,' Lonnie said. 'When I asked him, he said he was from a place called Corn Creek. I've never heard of it, have you?'

'I think so,' Thad Connely answered. 'Eastern Wyoming, I believe. Fifty miles or so out of Cheyenne.' Then the DL foreman rose, saying, 'I've had a long ride. If you folks will excuse me – Mr Link, Lonnie, Carla. I believe I'll turn in now.' He folded his napkin as well and placed it aside, patting Carla's shoulder lightly with the three fingers on his right hand.

After he was gone, Drew Link told his daughter, 'There goes a man who would love to have you, Carla. God knows why you would prefer to go off to San Francisco.'

Carla Link murmured, 'Yes, God knows.'

It was not the next day, but the day following that Kendo decided that he must rise from his bed or rot there, and so he dressed with extreme care and walked heavily out into the morning sunshine. There was a wooden chair on the small porch and he lowered himself into it to watch the ranch activities. A yellow dog walked to him, snuffled at his leg and went away, unimpressed. In the shade of a wide-spreading oak tree a tethered milk cow ate from a rick filled with new hay. A flock of brown chickens scratched aimlessly at the ground. Distantly, a hammer rang in the smithy's shop.

Everything about the DL Ranch indicated organization and prosperity. A yard man was sweeping off the porch of the big white house where Drew Link and his daughters lived. Two other men were wheeling a barrow loaded with firewood that way.

Kendo watched it all with trepidation. The time

must come when he was forced to walk up to the main house and confess to Drew Link that he had failed to deliver the herd of horses from Frank Pierce. The thought was depressing, even with the invigorating warmth of the new sun and the knowledge that the wound in his back was healing rapidly. A blue bird landed on the rail of the steps, studying him with a bright eye before darting away on stubby wings.

Why not get it over with? Kendo demanded of himself.

Likely Drew Link was growing apprehensive, wondering where the horses had got to. Confess and be damned! At least the man could then make plans to replace the horses. Determined, Kendo got to his feet, pausing for a moment to brace himself against the rail, breathing deeply, slowly. Then he started toward the big house. There was nothing left to lose of his reputation. May as well get it over with.

'It can't be him,' Oscar Campbell said, shaking his head heavily. The three, Thad Connely, Oscar Campbell and Tyler Morse stood together in the shadows of the oak tree. Morse, small, dark, with a cruelly scarred mouth, agreed.

'That's been years back, Thad.'

'I tell you . . . look, how many men have you met

named Kendo? And from Corn Creek? It's him. No doubt about it.'

Oscar Campbell shook his head again. Everything about the man was large and slow. His head moved from side to side heavily. 'Why? Thad, why would a man spend years following us?'

'Some men are built that way,' little Tyler Morse said. 'Remember Dallas Tripp? He spent six years hunting down the man who cheated him in a card game. Got him too. Down in Mexico.'

'He couldn't have recognized us anyway,' Oscar Campbell said, returning to the point at hand. We were masked.'

'You're right, of course,' Thad Connely agreed. 'But it's too much coincidence that he's here. You don't suppose he could have been with the trail herd? Didn't you get one of them in the back, Oscar? This Kendo showed up shot in the back.'

'That *hombre* went down dead,' Oscar said defensively, as if missing his mark branded him as unreliable.

'Well, it's one or the other – or both!' Thad Connely said. 'Either he's taken his time finding us from the Corn Creek robbery, or he was with the horse herd,' Connely said with quiet firmness. 'Either way, he's got to be taken care of. We're too close to what we've been working for to let some saddle tramp get in the way.'

Drew Link was not smiling when Kendo, his faded red shirt covering the bandaging on his torso was shown into his office by a nondescript, balding house man. The ranch owner looked up from one of the documents on his desk and nodded a greeting.

'You must be Kendo,' Drew Link said.

'I am. How are you, Mr Link?'

'Not bad,' the silver-haired man answered. His eyes were narrowed with curiosity. 'How can I help you?'

'I've come bearing bad news, I'm afraid,' Kendo said. He shifted his position. No matter how he tried to stand, his back still ached.

'Oh?' Link's expression did not change. He seemed to always expect the worst. 'Go ahead. What is it, exactly, Kendo?'

'The horses Frank Pierce was driving over here . . . I'm afraid they won't be arriving, Mr Link.'

'They won't?' Link said, with a quirk of a smile.

'No, sir,' Kendo answered. 'You see—' Confession was proving harder than he had anticipated.

'Kendo,' Link interrupted, 'you are laboring under some sort of misconception. The horses did arrive. The day before yesterday. Forty-seven ponies. Three lost along the trail.' He shuffled the papers on his desk. 'I paid the full four thousand dollars anyway, understanding that these things happen.'

'You paid. . . ?'

'To the trail boss. What was his name? I have it here on the receipt. A Mr Bo Chandler.'

Bo Chandler. Of course it made sense. Why drive the herd a long distance, searching for a new buyer when Drew Link was here and expecting to pay for the horses? Kendo sighed inwardly and said, 'I'm the man that Frank Pierce entrusted the herd to.'

'But you were—'

'Shot in the back along the trail.'

'And this Bo Chandler took over for you,' Drew Link said, with an understanding nod.

'Yes. But Chandler is not to be trusted.'

'He delivered the herd,' Link observed. 'And apparently Frank Pierce trusted him enough to allow him to accompany it.'

'I doubt,' Kendo said unhappily, 'that Pierce will ever see the money you gave to Bo Chandler.'

'But you can't know that,' Link pointed out. 'Look, Kendo, I can see that there is something between you and Chandler; I can't do anything about that. Not to sound hard-hearted, but I purchased those horses from Pierce. They were delivered. I paid for them. Sorry, but whatever Chandler may or may not do with the money is beyond my control. My conscience is clear.' There were signs of irritability in Link's manner and in his voice now. Perhaps he had decided that Kendo had only come to him to air a past grievance.

'You're right, of course,' Kendo said after awhile. 'It's just. . . .'

'Never mind,' Link said rising from his leather chair. 'Let's just assume the matter is closed unless we hear otherwise, shall we?'

'Yes.'

'For the time being, rest and get well, Kendo.'

'Your generosity is appreciated,' Kendo said honestly. 'You know I have nothing with which to pay you back.'

'We can settle that later. When you're well enough we can find some light yard work to keep you busy until you feel healthy enough to ride. If you feel that you owe me.'

'I do. I would be grateful if you'll let me stay for a while longer.'

Link laughed, not deeply, but openly. 'You've talked to Lonnie, I know. Well, she and I have the same philosophy. We don't throw out an injured dog . . . or man. The prairie's a harsh place for a wounded man, or one who's down on his luck.'

'I, it appears,' Kendo answered, 'am both. Thank you.'

'Mr Link,' Kendo asked, 'was there an old man

with long gray hair with the herd? And a kid with red hair?' Because if Darcy Pitt and Aaron Collier were both still alive and well, perhaps Bo Chandler made the decision to play it straight.

'Sorry,' Drew Link said, shaking his head, 'I didn't really pay much attention to the other riders.'

Escorting Kendo to the door, Link looped a casual arm across Kendo's shoulders. 'I will have to ask you to move out of the room you've been occupying and bunk with the rest of the men. My foreman is back, and the room is rightfully his.'

'Of course,' Kendo agreed.

'I'll have someone show you where to bunk,' Link said. Crossing the carpeted front room, Kendo saw Lonnie standing in front of the low-burning fire, her hands clasped behind her back. He started to say something to her, but did not. She watched him go with an inexplicable sadness in her blue eyes.

Outside it was cool and growing cooler. The stars were brittle and clear. A yard dog yelped at something and fell silent. Kendo crossed the yard. In the shadows of the big oak tree the man jumped him.

Arms fell across his chest and he was thrown to the ground. His attacker was quickly on him, throwing lefts and rights wildly. Kendo was struck in the face, in the ribs, on his injured shoulder. The man was faceless and brutal in the night shadows.

From the darkness a second man emerged, threw his arms around the attacking man and pulled him, squirming and cursing from Kendo. The newcomer spun the other man aside and, as he skulked off into the night, the new arrival leaned forward, extending a hand to Kendo.

'He didn't hurt you, I hope,' Thad Connely said.

'Didn't have time.'

'Must have mistaken you for someone else. We don't make a habit of jumping injured men on the DL.'

'Who was it?' Kendo asked, coming to his feet with Thad's assistance.

'I'm not sure; I'll find out, though. My name's Thad Connely. DL foreman.'

'Oh. It's your room I've been staying in,' Kendo said, dusting himself off.

'That's all right. I've been away. A man can only sleep one place at a time.'

'I'm clearing out. Mr Link said for me to find a place in the bunkhouse.'

'We can do that for you now,' Thad Connely said. 'Don't let this incident sour you on the DL. We're mostly a pretty good bunch of men. Except for Saturday night,' he added with a throttled laugh. Kendo smiled thinly. Together they turned toward the bunkhouse where he was shown a bare bunk and given two fresh blankets to settle into.

'Why'd you stop it?' Tyler Morse asked Thad in his room adjacent to the barracks. 'We don't want him hanging around, do we?'

Oscar Campbell was on Tyler's side. 'Something might tip him off, Thad. Your hand, for instance.'

Thad Connely studied his three-fingered hand and answered, 'How many men have you seen missing a thumb or a finger on the range, Oscar? Hundreds, I'd bet. If he remembers that at all from Corn Creek, it's of no significance. I don't want Kendo chased off, get me?'

'But, Thad. . . .' Joe Handy said imploringly.

'We're better off having him around us, so we know where we can get our hands on him when the time comes.' Grimly he added, 'We still have uses for the man – wait and see.'

SIX

Kendo stayed in bed until late afternoon the following day, but when he rose he was restless. Sleep that night came with difficulty. He was determined to be up and active the next morning. And so with the dawn he rose, tugged on his boots and reported to the small, balding yard boss, Joe Handy, to ask for some work assignment.

'Don't look like you're fit for much,' Handy said, looking up from his coffee.

'I'm not, I'm afraid,' Kendo admitted.

'Well . . . think you can tidy up the boss-man's stable a little?'

'I'll give it a try.'

Handy nodded. 'There's only the wagon team and three personal mounts kept there – the boss's and those of Miz Lonnie and Miz Carla. It shouldn't take much raking. Do that and curry the horses and we'll call it a day's work.'

The barn was clean and dry, the horses content. Kendo got to work cleaning up the overnight residue. Finished with that he began currying the animals. His back seemed to loosen up as he worked at a carefully measured pace. Outside of a new lump on his head from last night's encounter, he felt noticeably improved. Brushing the white horse with the gray mane and tail – Drew Link's personal mount – Kendo found himself frowning in consideration.

Why had that man jumped him the previous evening? He knew none of the men on the ranch, could have given no one cause to hold a grudge. Thad Connely had guessed that it was a mistake. Yet even in the dark. . . .

He wondered idly where the old gray mare had been put. He wasn't thrilled with the idea of riding the dowager, but his own horse was long gone, and sooner or later he would be forced to return to Frank Pierce's ranch, no matter what awaited him there. If Bo Chandler had in fact lived up to the bargain, Kendo would be welcomed as one returned from the dead. If, on the other hand, Chandler had absconded with the money, or worse claimed that Kendo must be the one who stole it, then his welcome would be far more hostile.

'You're going to rub the hair off that horse,' a small voice said behind him, and Kendo turned to find the small dark girl, Nita, standing there with two water buckets.

Kendo smiled. 'Yes, he's had enough,' he agreed, swatting the white horse on the rump. 'I just needed to get busy, feel useful.'

'I know. Lying up in bed isn't the picnic folks think.'

'You usually bring water to these horses?' Kendo asked, lifting one of them to pour into the receptacle in the white horse's stall.

'Not always, but a lot of the boys are out on the range today,' Nita said. She was watering the leggy roan which apparently belonged to one of the Link girls. She leaned on the partition, watching the pony dip its muzzle into the water. Her eyes were far away.

'Kendo, you have to ride out of here as soon as you're able,' she said suddenly, turning toward him.

'Yes,' he agreed, 'I do.' He was thinking of Frank Pierce. The girl obviously had something else in mind.

'This is not a good place,' she said, glancing toward the open stable door.

'No?'

'No,' she said, stepping forward to look up at him

intently. 'If you are wise you will leave as soon as possible.'

Puzzled by the urgency in Nita's voice, Kendo said, 'But you stay here.'

'I have no choice,' she replied. 'My father is dead. He is the one who brought me out here. What am I to do? Trade this job for one in Ambrose? Slinging hash? I do not have money to run away to a place like San Francisco.'

'Why would you want to go there?' Kendo asked, for something to say.

'Why? I do not,' the dark-eyed girl said, 'but it must be a better place than the DL.'

'Seems pleasant enough around here,' Kendo said. The girl made a disparaging sound.

'You do not know it. This ranch is hell on earth. Leave before it is proved to you.' Her breasts rose and fell with emotion beneath the white blouse she wore. She touched his arm briefly with her fingertips. 'They will prove it to you – and then it will be too late.'

'I don't really understand what you are saying,' Kendo admitted.

'My father did not understand at first, either,' Nita said, 'and now he is dead. You are with them or against them.'

Kendo was silent, thoughtful. 'Is that why Carla

Link is so anxious to go to San Francisco? Because this is a dangerous place?'

'Yes,' Nita said in a drawn-out, emphatic hiss. 'She has lived here most of her life, seen more than even I have. This is a bad place, Kendo. And unless you are bad as well, this is no place for you.'

A long shadow stained the straw-littered floor of the stable and they looked up to see Joe Handy watching them. 'They all watered, Nita?'

'Not yet,' she said, hastily snatching up the oak buckets. 'Pretty soon.'

Then she spun and walked out, brushing past the balding red-headed yard boss, fear seeming to compress her mouth.

'You, Kendo, how's it going?'

'Not bad. I'm a little sore, but mostly all right. Say, Joe, do you have any idea where that old gray mare I was riding might be?'

'No. I'll find out for you. It's probably in the old corral – that's about a quarter of a mile the other side of the big house.'

'Thanks,' Kendo said.

'Planning on riding out?' the yard boss enquired casually.

'Not today, that's for sure,' Kendo said with a laugh.

'Well, take care of yourself. Knock it off any time

you start to hurt.' Then Joe Handy turned and walked slowly away.

Kendo waited for a few minutes. He wanted to stay and talk with Nita some more. The girl was cryptic in her revelations, but he had no doubt that she was sincere. And that she was frightened of something that hung over the ranch.

Kendo went out and walked through the bright sunlight. The air was crisp, but only the faintest of breezes moved, barely enough to turn the leaves on the big oak trees. He went behind the big white house and continued on, noticing the shuttered windows. The big yellow yard dog he had seen before fell in behind him in companionable silence.

Kendo pondered as he walked. Joe Handy had referred to the pen where the gray mare probably was located as 'the old corral'. That indicated that there was a newer pen as well. He wanted to find it if possible. He wanted to have a look at the horses. He needed to know if Drew Link had actually taken possession of the herd Frank Pierce had sent along.

Accompanied still by the big dog, Kendo found the corral. In it was the old gray mare and a few other misfits. A shaggy dun pony, two yearlings and a second mare – a pinto – among them. Obviously this was not the riding stock. The gray mare wandered over to meet Kendo, thrusting her muzzle toward him. He stroked the patient animal's neck while his eyes searched the land which was short-grass range broken by stands of live oak and closer to the creek, willow and sycamores. He saw no sign of a second corral. Was it hidden somewhere? And if so *why*?

At the sound of approaching horses, Kendo turned to see Thad Connely and a thick, red-faced man riding toward him. Neither was smiling.

'Finding your way around?' Connely asked, reining his black horse in.

'Wanted to find my old mare.'

'Why?' the other man asked disparagingly, studying the gray. 'Short on dog meat?'

'Be polite, Oscar,' Thad Connely said, although he was smiling. 'Every man to his own taste.'

'She's all the transportation I have left,' Kendo explained. He took no offense at Oscar Campbell's crack. 'If you should happen to run across a saddled four-year old gray with a blaze, it's mine.'

'Still saddled?' Campbell said, frowning.

'It was when someone back-shot me,' Kendo said, and now he was not smiling, nor were Campbell and Thad Connely. 'It might have found its way back to the herd.'

'If we run across it, we'll let you know,' Thad Connely said thinly.

'I was thinking it might be here . . . or in the other

corral,' Kendo said.

The DL riders exchanged a glance. Connely muttered his reply, 'Doubt it.'

The two turned their horses and continued on their way. Kendo watched after them as they faded into the distance. Their manner had been neither hostile, nor overly friendly, but Kendo had sensed an underlying current. He did not place complete faith in Nita's assertion that the DL was 'a bad place', but he had certainly felt more comfortable in other places. As soon as he felt that he was capable of sitting in the saddle for ten hours a day, he would be gone anyway.

He had other demons to face.

Moved into the barracks proper, Kendo felt even more ill at ease. The hands there seemed to resent his presence. He lay on his bunk, speaking to no one, not being spoken to. He felt a stranger in a strange land. The conversations around him were muted, accompanied by sidelong glances at his cot. This in itself was unusual. He had been around cowboys most of his life. Usually they were a boisterous, rowdy lot. These men, when they gambled, placed the cards down carefully; when they drank, they did so in silence, not exchanging jokes or trail stories.

Sometime hours after sunset, he rose stiffly from

his bed and slipped out into the yard. If he thought his battered body could manage it, he would have ridden out of the DL Ranch at that moment, bareback on the old gray mare. But he could not, and knew it.

He wandered through the moon-shadows of the old oak trees and came suddenly upon Lonnie Link. The blonde was startled by his approach. It was obvious that she had been expecting someone else.

'Can't sleep?' she asked with forced cheerfulness.

'No.'

'If you're still in that much pain. . . .'

'It's not that. Thanks, Lonnie.'

'Sure.'

'Well, then,' he said awkwardly, 'good evening.' He touched the fingers of his right hand to where the brim of his hat would have been had he been wearing one and walked away slowly. A few minutes later he passed Thad Connely who was walking rapidly toward the spot where Kendo had left Lonnie. Connely said nothing. Only nodding, he continued on his way, with one malevolent backward glance.

Now what was that about? Kendo wondered.

As he understood things it was Carla Link who held Thad's interest, and he hers. Well, there could be dozens of reasons a ranch foreman would want to talk to one of the owner's daughters; they did not necessarily have to be romantic in nature. What of it, if it were so? It meant nothing to Kendo. Let the three of them sort it out.

All that he wanted to do now was try to get a good night's sleep and let his body heal a little more before striking out. It was not to be.

Again a man's shadow emerged from the night trees and launched himself at Kendo. Kendo was alert enough to side step and the attacker only grazed him with a wildly-thrown right hand. Still he staggered back from the force of the glancing blow. There was no doubt in his mind that it was the same man who had jumped him the previous night. The man crouched the same, *smelled* the same. He wore a pale yellow shirt and black jeans. There was enough moonlight beaming through the foliage of the oaks for Kendo to make out his face on this night.

They called him Tyler Morse, a dark man with a badly scarred mouth, one Kendo had taken for a close friend of Thad Connely. Why the cowboy should wish to attack him, he could not guess, but that was what he again had in mind as he circled Kendo, both fists bunched tightly. Kendo was still in no shape for an all-out brawl, but he felt a little stronger, a little more capable of defending himself on this night. As Tyler Morse came in carelessly, Kendo jabbed his left into the smaller man's face. Blood began to trickle from Morse's nose and he wiped it away with a curse.

Still moving in a crouch, still circling, Morse tried it again. Kendo, even in bad shape, was not the easy mark Morse had taken him for when he jumped him and threw him down the previous night. Morse swung wildly, all of his blows arcing wide. Kendo was no boxer, but he had been taught to shoot straight rights and lefts. These blows had more power behind them and were more accurate than Morse's looping attempts.

In the small moonlit clearing both men circled. Kendo managed to get up on his toes and jab the shorter man as they moved. The straight lefts sent Morse's head rocking back. A forceful right split Tyler Morse's cheek open and the man bawled out in anger.

Morse didn't have the heart for it. Or the skills. Muttering vague threats, he lowered his hands in a gesture of surrender and stalked away through the tangled shadows, leaving Kendo to ponder. He had done nothing to Morse, barely knew the man. If Morse was not trying to settle a dispute, which he could not have been, then he was simply trying to make life tough for Kendo, perhaps to drive him away.

Why? The only possible reason Kendo could come

up with was his curiosity about the horses in the 'new' corral which he had so far been unable to locate. Yet Drew Link had told him, honestly or not, that he had purchased Frank Pierce's herd, paid Bo Chandler and seen him on his way. What could it possibly matter then if Kendo spotted familiar horse flesh?

The pain in Kendo's shoulder had flared up again. His back continued to ache. He made his determination. It was not in surrender to Tyler Morse's tactics, nor out of any fear at all, but he was going to ride out – that very night. What was he hoping to accomplish on the DL? The ride would be slow; he would need to stop and rest often along the trail, but he was going back to the Pierce Ranch.

Let the DL keep its secrets; he wanted to know nothing more about them.

Kendo returned to the bunkhouse, glanced around for Morse, but did not see him. Other men stood in groups or sat at the table playing cards and drinking whiskey. These turned mocking or spiteful eyes his way, but no man said a word. Kendo walked to his bunk, snatched his hat from the bedpost and went out again, slamming the door behind him.

The hell with them all. They wanted him gone; he was going.

The night had grown cooler. A silver dollar moon

surrounded by a thousand bright stars hung in the dark sky. Kendo walked past the big house, making his way toward the old corral. The gray mare certainly wasn't his first choice as a mount, but she was reliable – and she was his! No man could challenge his right to ownership. She had been no part of the sale agreement.

Kendo saw no man standing watch. The mare, recognizing him even in the night, clomped over to greet him. Kendo wished for a saddle, but he would rather be away from the DL than beg for gear.

Perhaps things were well on the Pierce Ranch after all, perhaps Bo Chandler had returned with the money from the sale. Perhaps . . . but Kendo seriously doubted it.

Unfastening the wire loop that held one post to the other, Kendo swung the gate wide to allow the gray mare to come out. A few of the other horses seemed inclined to follow and so Kendo swung the gate to quickly.

'Well,' Kendo said, with unhappy fondness as he stroked the mare's muzzle, 'here we go again.'

'Without so much as a saddle?' the feminine voice asked from behind him. He turned slowly to find an unexpected visitor. Carla Link.

'Surprised to see you here,' he said.

'I've got my sorrel back in the trees,' she said in a

throaty whisper. 'Can you see me as far as Ambrose?'

'Are you crazy?' Kendo asked with a tight laugh. The blonde came nearer. Moonlight smoothed her sometimes harsh features. She looked more ... womanish on this night.

'Crazy?' Carla repeated, 'I must be. Look at how many years I've spent on the DL.'

'But you were going to leave soon. For San Francisco,' Kendo said, watching the house and surrounding country for any arriving riders. He did not like the feel of matters. Nor did he entirely trust the girl.

'I *was* going to San Francisco. To get away from this madness. I thought I had finally gotten my way, but Father has changed his mind. Lonnie and Thad Connely talked to him this evening. I don't know what was said, but the trip is off.'

'What, then, will you do?' Kendo asked. 'Surely there's nothing for you in Ambrose.'

'I will go there first. I have a little money of my own. Enough to get away. Do you know, Kendo, how important it is sometimes to just get *away*, even when you have no particular destiny in mind?'

'I think I do,' he had to admit. 'Get your horse and make it quick. I can at least see you into Ambrose if you're that determined.'

And if Drew Link didn't catch up, an enraged

father. Or Thad Connely, a jilted lover. Or . . . damnation. It seemed that you could leave the DL, but you couldn't get away from it.

It didn't take long for Carla Link to catch up her sorrel pony and return. Nor for the other rider to emerge from the shadows and approach them as they prepared to make their run.

SEVEN

'I'm going too,' Nita said to Carla Link. 'If you're brave enough to try it, so am I.'

The frown that had been deepening on Kendo's face since Carla Link had appeared out of the night now became set and stony. Now he was expected to escort two crazy women to Ambrose – which was far off his intended course anyway.

'Do either of you two know what you are up to?' Kendo asked grumpily.

'Yes, we do,' Nita said, turning her dark eyes up to him. 'And it is best if we do it quickly, isn't it?'

Kendo hesitated, started to answer and then grasped the gray mare's mane. Nita interrupted his movements. 'I know where your horse is, Kendo.'

'My horse?'

'A steel gray gelding with a white blaze, is it not?

When it was collected up, it was still wearing a saddle. Isn't that your horse?'

'Yes,' Kendo said, 'it is.'

'I saw it over in the new corral. Someone said that you asked Thad Connely to keep an eye out for it. It's there, and the last time I saw it, your saddle was there as well, thrown over a corral bar.'

'Show me,' Kendo said. 'Is anyone standing watch?'

'I don't think so. There isn't normally. It would speed us up, wouldn't it – if we can get your horse?'

'It would,' he replied. The relative luxury of a saddle compared to sitting on the mare's spine for days was an irresistible magnet.

'What about this old girl?' Carla Link asked with unexpected sympathy.

'She'll follow along – at her own speed. If she can't keep up, well, the graze in this part of the country will be plenty to keep her.'

They started along the path, Nita leading the way, Kendo walking beside Carla's horse. A few minutes later, Carla asked, 'Have you had that pistol on your hip the whole time you were here?'

'Why do you ask? Of course I have. Except for when I left it in Thad's room to visit your father.'

'I'd check my loads if I were you,' Carla said meaningfully.

'You don't mean. . . .' Kendo stopped dead, snaked his Colt from its holster and cursed softly. 'Empty. How did you know?'

'It's not a new trick. Not around here.'

Shaking his head, Kendo removed fresh cartridges from his belt loops and thumbed them into the cylinder of the Colt.

'If you'd made trouble,' Carla said as they started one, 'someone would have goaded you into a shooting match.'

Kendo shook his head in disbelief. Apparently there was still much he did not know about the DL. Much he did not wish to know. But he understood Nita's assessment now. The DL was a bad place indeed for strangers.

The moon glossed the backs of half a hundred horses in a long, broad corral. Standing on a middle rail, Kendo looked for and eventually spotted his gray horse. His saddle and bridle he had already seen thrown over a top rung of the log enclosure.

'I'll get him,' Kendo said. 'Keep watch, will you?'

'Do you need a rope?' Nita asked.

'No, not for him,' Kendo told her.

He moved past the heated bodies of the horses, recognizing many of them from Pierce's stock, including the big shaggy buckskin with its contrary ways. And. . . .

Darcy Pitt's piebald pony was there as well. He could not spot Aaron Collier's little sorrel among the milling herd, but he had no doubt that it, too, was there. Then Bo Chandler had taken care of business. Or had the DL crew – or both, worked in concert? There was no way of knowing, and just then Kendo spared it no more speculation. He only knew that he wanted to get off of DL range as soon as possible.

'Hold that gate, will you?' Kendo said. His voice sounding unnaturally loud in the charged night. From horseback, Nita swung the gate to the corral open and swung it shut as he led his big steel gray gelding out. In minutes he had slipped the horse its bit and tightened the double cinches on his Texas-style saddle.

Then they were off: Kendo and the two crazy ladies. Riding . . . away. And as rapidly as possible.

'I can't see the mare,' Carla said once, as they trotted their ponies north toward Ambrose.

'She'll be along,' Kendo said. And if not, it did not matter much. If the old mare tired, she would find herself free and standing with good graze for miles around. There were other things to worry about than the mare. How long would it take for Link to discover that his daughter had gone? For Thad Connely to find that his woman had ridden off with another man? And what would each imagine? Retribution could be minutes behind them, Kendo knew and he rode with unusual haste and rising apprehension.

At first he took the glow in the sky for dawn light, but it was too diffused, obviously glimmering in the north and not the east. Ambrose lay slumped and sadly unappealing ahead, circled by shadowed hills.

'Thank God,' Carla said, in an over-loud voice.

'Keep riding,' Kendo said, glancing across his shoulder. 'We're not there yet.'

Within half an hour they were. How the rutted streets of the miserable little frontier town could seem so welcome and comforting was difficult to explain, but they each felt safer than they had in a long while. Carla had indeed been carrying some getaway money with her, and they settled into two rooms in the hotel, Carla and Nita sharing one. Before the women turned in for the night, Kendo knocked at the door. There were still things he had to know.

The lantern was burning low. Both women had their hair unpinned, though both were fully dressed. Carla continued to brush her golden hair as they spoke. Perched on the edge of the bed, Kendo got to the point.

'What's really going on out on the DL?' he asked. Carla was seated on a chair before the mirror, Nita was leaning against the wall next to the window, her arms crossed beneath her breasts. The window was open a crack and the night breeze stirred the sheer curtains.

Nita answered explosively, 'It's an outlaw camp! Nothing more than a criminal enterprise.'

Carla, as was to be expected, was kinder in her explanation, 'It's a ranch that lost its way,' she said, placing her hair brush aside.

'What does that mean?' Kendo asked.

'It's a hard land,' Carla said thoughtfully. 'My father struggled for years. When we were young, Lonnie and I could not be sure we'd have an evening meal, or socks to wear when it was cold. It looked like the ranch was headed for broke. Men started to come by,' she went on, 'and they would offer large sums for a place to stay.'

'To hide out,' Nita put in angrily. Carla shrugged slightly.

'Sometimes these men would ride out for days, weeks, and then return, always wealthier than when they left. Father knew but did not want to know, if you understand me,' she said to Kendo. He said that he did.

'They returned with gifts – cattle sometimes, or horses, sometimes with cash money so that Lonnie and I could afford all of the things we needed. And it . . .' she faltered, 'sort of continued.'

'You failed to mention that men were killed there,' Nita said, angry now. 'My father, when he objected.'

'That was over you!' Carla retorted.

'No,' Nita said heavily. 'The men never bothered me. They would make rude comments, sometimes make a grab at me as I passed, but they were only showing off for their friends. My father was shot to death because he threatened to tell the law what was happening on the DL.'

Carla started to object, did not and closed her mouth. It seemed she did not want to admit that her father was in the wrong but could no longer avoid the fact that he was.

'Is all this why you wanted to go to San Francisco?' Kendo asked the blonde.

'Yes,' she admitted and her head hung a little. 'I wanted to go *anywhere.* This time I had father's promise. He had come into a large chunk of money – I knew where it had come from, but I didn't care anymore, I had to get away!'

'He changed his mind.'

'Lonnie and Thad Connely changed it for him, I told you that. Because Thad wants to marry me. Because Father had said that I could go only if my sister went with me as a companion. And she would never leave the DL.'

'If it's that bad. . . .' Kendo said.

'It's that bad!' Carla Link said sharply. 'Also, it is a place where a clever woman like Lonnie could grow immensely wealthy. That,' she finished with bitter sadness, 'is what Lonnie wants. The money that flows through the DL.'

'When she came to take me out there, to help me. . . .' Kendo began uneasily.

'Lonnie has never done a thing in her adult life just for the sake of helping someone. Thad instructed her to come into town and bring you back to the ranch. They didn't want you talking about the horse herd. You were supposed to have been killed back along the trail.'

Kendo nodded, lifted his eyes and asked, 'Who shot me?'

'I don't know,' Carla said throwing one hand skyward in frustration. 'It could have been any of them. Whoever's turn it was to do the next murder.'

After a long minute which passed with no sounds but muted voices of cowboys hooting in the far-off saloon, Kendo asked, 'What about Bo Chandler? Did he actually get paid for the horses, or is he a part of the gang?'

'I don't know. I can't imagine them actually giving Chandler the money. Perhaps they split it in a way that satisfied everybody.'

'You're probably right,' Kendo said, getting to his

feet. 'You ladies look about done in and my back is starting to pain me again. For tonight, let's leave things as they are, shall we? I want to be riding early, and I suppose you two have your plans to make as well.'

'Yes,' Carla said. She also had risen. 'I'm going to take a coach somewhere – Portland, Denver – I don't care where. The first one to leave in the morning, no matter its destination. From wherever it is, I'll make my way to California.'

'You'll be going along, Nita?' Kendo asked.

'Me?' Nita looked his way, half-smiled and shook her head. 'I told you. I don't want to go to San Francisco. What's there for me?'

'You mean to stay here?' Kendo asked in disbelief. 'In Ambrose?'

'No, Kendo,' Nita said. She turned her back to him before she completed her thought. 'I figure I'll just ride along with you.'

'You can't be—'

Carla interrupted. She put a hand on Kendo's shoulder and said, 'As you suggested, for tonight let's leave things as they are.'

Kendo returned to his room, tugged off his boots and tossed his hat on to the wooden chair. He lay back, needing sleep to soothe his aching back, but sleep did not come easily. He still had to worry about

Frank Pierce's lost herd, Bo Chandler and all of the DL – once Link realized his daughter was gone, he would hit the trail with a gang of men to bring her back. These were tangled, worrying thoughts and Kendo could not yet sort out all of the implications they carried. There was all of that. . . .

And Nita besides.

'Didn't I tell you to leave him alone!' a hostile Thad Connely shouted. He pushed Tyler Morse up against the outside wall of the barracks so hard that the breath was driven out of the smaller man. His badly scarred lips showed fresh bruising and his cheek was split open. There was no way for Tyler to deny that he had been fighting, and with Kendo gone from his bunk, it was obvious who he had tangled with.

Tyler eyes were wide with fear, 'I swear I didn't—'

'You didn't what? Think you had to listen to me!' Thad Connely's hand tightened around the bunched fabric of Tyler Morse's shirt front and then loosened again. What was the point in it? Angrily he pushed Morse aside. 'You knew I wanted him kept on the DL.'

'I don't see why,' Morse said breathlessly.

'Because you're an idiot. Worse, an idiot who doesn't listen!' Thad Connely deliberately slowed his breathing. 'He was looking for the horses, wasn't he?

If he snooped around enough to find out what really happened in the 'sale', who knows what he might have done? Certainly ridden back to report things to Frank Pierce. Which seems to be exactly where he is heading.'

'What can Pierce do?' Morse objected. 'He's an old man – he doesn't have that many hands on his ranch.'

'Have you been there, Tyler? Do you know that? Have you ever heard of hiring extra men! If Pierce were mad enough at being taken he might even go to the law. Then the DL wouldn't even exist anymore, and we'd be out on the range living out of our saddle-bags like we did in the early days – all thanks to you!'

'I guess I just wasn't thinking, Thad.'

'Shut up.'

'I just wanted to remind Kendo not to talk about Corn Creek.'

'Will you forget Corn Creek!' an exasperated Thad Connely shouted. 'That's been so long ago, and anyway we were all wearing masks. If you had just laid off another couple of days, I would have seen to it that Kendo was removed silently. I would have told Drew Link that he just rode away, saying nothing.

'Now,' Thad exploded, building up a fresh head of steam, 'he's gone all right! And he's taken Carla with him.'

'We'll find him,' Tyler Morse said.

'Oh, we'll find him,' Thad Connely said. 'Will that be before or after he's reported what happened on the DL? Before or after Carla's disappeared? Or maybe she won't disappear at all. Maybe the girl will decide that she has some talking to do, too. And if she ever talked, with all she knows. . . .' Thad Connely didn't remember drawing his Colt revolver, but now he had the cold blue steel of its muzzle pressed roughly against Tyler Morse's throat.

'I ought to blow your head off,' Thad muttered, but after a long minute as the sweating Tyler Morse wriggled and seemed to shrink before his eyes, Thad holstered the pistol, spun and stalked off toward the big house. Tyler Morse was having second thoughts now. He rubbed his throat and considered.

Maybe it wouldn't be that bad an idea if he just rode out himself.

'Well?' Lonnie Link demanded, as she met Thad Connely on the front porch of the big white house.

'Well what? They're gone. The three of them.'

'We've got to ride after them,' Lonnie said fiercely. Her blue eyes were fiery in the dim glow of the porch light.

'We can't track anyone in the dark,' Thad answered pragmatically.

'They must have gone to Ambrose.'

'Probably, though I don't know why Kendo would want to ride that way, it being off his course. But if you're wrong, Lonnie, we could find ourselves on tired horses, miles away from their trail. There's nothing to do but wait till daylight.'

In exasperation, the blonde said, 'All right. I'll be ready then.'

'What's the point in you going?' Thad Connely asked.

'You think I want to stay around and explain it all to my father?' she demanded. 'Besides' – her eyes grew feral – 'I don't think any of you has the guts to shoot down a woman.'

Lonnie undressed leisurely and slid into her canopied bed. She yawned and stretched luxuriously. She would sleep well on this night; she always did. Let the men do the worrying. Ever since she had been old enough to understand the business of the DL, Lonnie had recognized that the empire would one day be hers, and that it must remain profitable.

Men took to her immediately; they always had. Thad Connely was no cleverer in that sense than any of the rest of them, but he had a canny streak of criminality about him. He wanted the same thing she did – more. He had played his part of a suitor for

Carla's hand well, but Carla had not reciprocated. Perhaps she had seen beneath the suaveness to the serpent's heart within. Who knew? But Carla was insistent about wishing to leave the DL, not content with the leisure and wealth it provided. Carla seemed to walk in fear.

Lonnie Link did not know the meaning of fear.

She knew only that Carla, on the loose, was not to be trusted to keep the DL's secrets. Suppose one day she decided to tell all she knew? The wreckage would be complete. Lonnie could not let that happen.

Her father was beginning to show his age. Drew Link was no longer one to be concerned about. Besides, Lonnie had him wrapped around her little finger. Thad Connely might become a problem one day. He saw himself as Lonnie's equal partner and heir-apparent to the DL. Of course he was not; she would not allow it. If he ever began to think himself more important than he was, well he could always be eliminated. She would not have to do it herself.

There was always another man to do her bidding.

Carla was a different story. She had to be stopped and now. And what Lonnie had said to Thad Connely was true enough: she doubted if even these hard-bitten outlaws would be willing to pull the trigger on a woman.

She, herself, had no such qualms. She did not

allow such weaknesses.

Sorry, Carla, Lonnie thought, *but you have disappointed me.*

EIGHT

'You mustn't tell them where I've gone. No matter what!' Carla was frantic. Perhaps she only now realized the repercussions of what she was doing. Nita glanced at Kendo who stood before the flaming morning sky shining through the small hotel window. Nita was calming Carla Link.

'You don't have to worry. We won't say a word. When we start riding, they'll probably think that it's you and Kendo riding together, that I'm the one who's taken the westbound stage,' Nita said calmly.

'Yes,' Carla said, still over-excited, 'yes, I suppose you're right. That's probably what they will think.'

Kendo tried his hand at reassuring the blonde. 'Your coach leaves at eight. Unless they rode overnight – and they can't have or they'd be here by now – you'll be long gone before they reach

Ambrose. Once you're on board the stagecoach, you'll have the other passengers, the driver and shotgun rider surrounding you. They'll never catch you, Carla. You're safe now.'

Did he believe that? Not entirely. A check with the ticket agent would give them a description that could only match Carla. Who knew if there would even be any other passengers, or if the shotgun rider would be willing to fight the ten or more men Thad could easily muster once he realized that they wanted no valuables but only to return a runaway girl to her family? There was no certainty – our lives are based on chance and vagaries to a large part – but Kendo believed that Carla would make it safely away.

Of his own chances, he was not so certain.

Morning grew bright and clear, with only a few distant white clouds roaming across the sky. Nita and Kendo stood watching as the stagecoach departed Ambrose, dust swirling up in its wake.

'Well, that's that,' Kendo said, as they started back toward the stable where they had left their horses.

'Yes,' Nita said. She wore blue jeans and a faded blue shirt, a Stetson on her head. Her dark eyes were filled with quiet emotion.

'Did she tell you how far that ticket is taking her?' Kendo asked.

'No.'

'Well, that's probably for the best,' Kendo said. He realized that he was talking just to be talking. A sort of nervous tension had settled between them. 'I still think you should have gone with her.'

'What for?' Nita shrugged. 'Where she is going I do not wish to go. I am not a city girl.'

He halted where the boardwalk ended just before the stable was reached. 'You could still look around for a job, here in Ambrose.'

'Yes,' she said, drawing out the word. 'The DL riders would never find me here. Do you think, Kendo, that they wanted me off the ranch any more than they did Carla? I know a lot, too. They will fear that one day I might say the wrong thing to the wrong people.'

'I suppose you're right,' he admitted.

'I have been a prisoner, Kendo. I will not be taken back there.'

'It's not a good idea to ride with me,' Kendo said, growing more definite.

'You are the only honest man I have met since my father died – was murdered,' Nita said, lifting those liquid eyes to his. 'I trust you to take me away from here.'

Kendo tried again. 'Nita, I am riding into trouble.'

'Worse trouble than on the DL?' she asked.

Kendo thought of Frank Pierce, of Bo Chandler,

McColl and Charlie Weeks. It was trouble going back there, but not so much trouble as he had on the DL surrounded by dozens of thieves and gunmen. He did not answer directly.

'Come on, then,' he growled. 'Let's make tracks out of here before they catch up.'

The one advantage that they did have – assuming that logic would eventually lead the DL riders to Ambrose, was that their own ponies were now well rested, and the outlaws' horses would be exhausted after the long ride. It was best to use that advantage to its fullest now, and put some miles between them and the followers.

Carla's sorrel they left at the stable. Kendo thought it a good idea to make it seem that the Link girl had acted alone. Besides, there was the matter of being caught and possibly accused of having stolen the horse. That was a hanging offense in a country where a man afoot was a dead man.

The stableman helped Nita saddle her dun pony. Kendo found that his back was sufficiently healed so that the job of saddling his own gray was relatively pain free. Walking their ponies to a general store they purchased a few provisions, filled their canteens from a pump, and began their uncertain journey.

The sun was low in their eyes, beaming through a stand of cottonwoods as they started on their way.

Kendo found it a pleasure to again be sitting on his own horse. Nita was silent, not sullen, but simply quiet as they crossed a silvery rill and began their long trek across the limitless plains.

'Where are we going?' Nita asked after another mile.

'Didn't I tell you? There's a man named Frank Pierce. Those horses were his. I have to go back to his ranch, find out if he ever received the money for the sale. If not, well, I am the one to blame.'

'Then why return to—?'

'I have to face him, that's all!' Kendo said sharply. Corn Creek still haunted him.

Kendo's idea was to retrace the route they had followed westward. He wanted to see if he could find the bodies of Darcy Pitt and Aaron Collier, any other evidence the horse thieves might have left behind them. Something that might prove to Pierce that he was not the guilty party in the affair.

'You didn't hear anything about how much money was to be paid, or to whom?' Kendo asked.

'I was not party to any discussion like that,' Nita said. 'Why would they want me around?'

'It was just a faint hope,' Kendo said. 'If you had overheard anything—'

Kendo's voice broke off. He raised a hand to halt Nita. Drawing his pistol, he sat the shying gray horse, his eyes fixed on a low gully ahead.

'What is it?' Nita whispered.

'Something moved in the willow brush over there. Could be a cougar, coyote . . . might have been a man.'

'A man would have called out.'

'Not if he was up to no good. Hold my horse,' Kendo said, and he crossed his right leg over the steel-gray's neck to slide to the ground. As Nita watched, Kendo, Colt in hand, moved southward fifty feet or so and then disappeared into the gully himself. She watched and waited for gunshots to ring out, for a man to die.

Kendo moved like a cat through the screen of willow brush clotting the narrow wash. This might all be foolishness. As he had told Nita, it could simply be some wild creature that had caused the brush to shift. But if it was a man, they simply could not ride on past and give a bushwhacker a chance to pick them off from behind. It was not a warm day, but in the wash where not a trace of breeze reached, Kendo found perspiration beginning to bead his forehead and trickle down his throat. The revolver in his hand was slick with sweat. He paused, wiped his hand on his jeans and continued, his boots soundless against the sandy bottom of the gully.

'That's close enough,' a voice from the dense

willow brush said, and Kendo froze.

Something in his memory was jogged by the voice. He thought for a moment that he had recognized it. It couldn't be, could it? He called out cautiously, 'Darcy? Darcy Pitt?'

'Who's that?'

'Kendo.'

'Kendo! I thought you were long dead. You took your time finding me!' Relief and anguish were mingled in the words.

'Can I come along?'

'Come forward. Are you alone?'

'Yes,' Kendo answered and he swept brush away with his left arm as he wove through the thicket. He eventually found the place where Darcy Pitt had chosen to make his last stand. Against the sandy soil the old trailsman lay, his face criss-crossed by the shadows of the willows. His smile was wan, his eyes pouched and bloodshot. A rag was knotted clumsily around his head. Dried purple blood caked the side of his head. His Henry repeating rifle was clenched in his hands.

'So they didn't get you after all,' Pitt commented, as Kendo crouched down beside him.

'Oh, they got me,' Kendo replied. 'That's what's taken me so long.'

'I'm damnably hungry,' Pitt said as Kendo sat him

up. 'I only had a rabbit and a rattlesnake – both raw – to eat in the last three days. I had water from the puddles the rain left, but that's been soaked up by the ground now.'

'We've got food and water,' Kendo said. 'Where did they get you, Darcy?'

'*We*?' Darcy Pitt said suspiciously, 'I thought you said that you were alone.'

'It's no one you have to worry about,' Kendo said soothingly. 'Come on, let's get you to your feet.'

Darcy showed no surprise when they returned to the horses to find Nita standing beside her dun pony, still holding the reins to the steel-dust gray, but he must have been confused by her sudden appearance. After all, this was a wild land, a man's land and women, especially young pretty women, were few and far between.

The old plainsman only asked, 'Where'd you catch her?'

'Darcy, this is Nita. Nita, Darcy Pitt. He was riding with me when the herd was taken.'

' 'Lo, Miss,' Pitt muttered. The grizzled old trailsman seemed embarrassed. His long gray hair hung free, his face was scabbed. Perhaps he thought that he was not at his best to present himself to a lady.

'I need to talk to you,' Kendo said to Darcy, 'about

what happened back then. I was shot and saw none of it.'

'How about we talk while we ride?' Darcy suggested. 'I've developed a sudden disliking for the open spaces.'

'All right,' Kendo agreed. 'I guess Nita can ride up behind me and you can have the dun, or—'

'What's the matter with Grandma there?' Pitt asked, inclining his head.

'With. . . ?' The plodding old gray mare had caught up with them. She stood twenty feet off, watching them with what seemed to be accusing eyes. It was as if she were asking how they could have just ridden off and left her after all she had tried to do for them.

'Nothing,' Kendo said, 'except she's slow as molasses. If you can ride her bareback. . . .'

'Son,' Pitt told Kendo, 'when I was a younger man I rode a bull buffalo on a bet.'

That settled, they started on again as the sun rose higher and the rising wind flattened the long grass, the miles of it stretching out in all directions. A golden eagle circled high overhead as if watching them with curiosity. What it was watching became obvious as it dove, disappeared for a few seconds and took to wing again with a brush rabbit in its talons.

'How'd they get you, Pitt?' Kendo asked, as the two

rode side by side. Nita held back a little way, her head constantly swiveling to watch the back trail.

'Pretty girl,' Pitt commented before he replied, 'one thing I regret about growing older you just become invisible to them. What happened,' he went on with a sigh, 'was that it started to rain, as you know. I started for Pocono Springs, hoping the boys might have thrown up some kind of shelter. What I found instead was six or seven new riders discussing something with Bo Chandler. I knew something was up. Hatha was gone, you were missing and these *hombres* were in camp. We always suspected, you and me, that there was going to be trouble on the trail, and here it was.'

Darcy Pitt went on, 'Not liking the looks of things I held back. Suddenly I saw a man's hand lift, a finger point at me, and someone shot. A bullet clipped my skull. I gave my heels to the piebald and we went racing away as the storm began to get terrible heavy. A dizziness came over me. I couldn't stay in the saddle. I fell, crawled away and lay waiting for them. Except I soon passed out and I couldn't have done a thing if they had tracked me. The rain was so heavy, I doubt it could have been done on that night, and I figure they were in a hurry to get wherever they were going. I don't know what happened to my piebald. I kept hoping it might come back.'

'It went back to the herd. I saw it just yesterday. What happened to Aaron Collier?' Kendo wanted to know.

Pitt shook his head. 'I don't know. I didn't see him then and haven't since. You have to figure that they plugged him.'

'If—' Kendo began but he was interrupted by a sharp yell from Nita.

'Kendo! They're coming,' she called as she kneed her dun pony toward them.

'They can't have caught up,' Kendo said, squinting toward the eastern horizon.

'You'd better tell them that,' Nita said shakily. 'Because it sure looks to me as if they have. And that lead horse is sure-hell Drew Link's white stallion.'

'Let's find some cover,' Kendo said grimly. Glancing at the old mare Pitt was sitting, he added, 'We aren't going to outrun them.'

'Is there going to be shooting?' Nita asked. Her troubled eyes studied Kendo's set features.

'There sure is,' Kendo said. 'They won't hurt you, Nita – if you want to wait here for them to catch up. If that's Drew Link leading them, I'm sure he'd take you back.'

'Kendo,' Nita said, 'that is the one thing I cannot do – go back.'

'We'd better make some sort of plan, Kendo.' Pitt

was watching the approaching horsemen, still small dark figures against the horizon, but coming fast.

'You have something in mind?' Kendo asked, as they started their horses on a quickened pace. Ahead they saw another of the narrow gullies that scarred the countryside. Typically willow-clotted, it was one he recalled from the ride west. They were not now more than half a mile from Pocono Springs, he knew.

Pitt's words were harshly emphasized as the mare plodded heavily along at her strongest pace – which was not much. 'I figure . . . I can. . . .'

What Kendo eventually got from Darcy Pitt's words was that he meant to drop from the mare and take cover in the gully. There he could cover their retreat with his long gun.

'They'll be suspicious when they spot the mare with no rider,' Kendo shouted.

'No . . . won't,' Darcy insisted. No man had ridden away from the DL on the mare. She was a known herd-follower and had just tagged along. They could not know that Darcy Pitt had been found along the trail.

'All right,' Kendo said, as they again slowed their horses as they approached the sandy wash. 'Find your station.'

The trailing riders were closing distance rapidly,

although Kendo did not know how that could be, the DL mounts having run longer than their own horses. Nevertheless it was so. 'Kendo!' Nita said, and there was fear in her dark eyes now.

'We'll have to take cover too,' he said, pulling up his steel gray. 'We're in rifle range for them.'

They watched as Pitt scurried into the brush at the northern end of the dogleg the wash formed here. Kendo decided to go to the south. With luck, they would have the DL riders in a cross-fire position, and they could do some damage.

Kendo dismounted before his horse had stopped and waited to help Nita from the back of her dun. Taking her hand they raced for the gully as the DL rifles opened up, racketing across the plains.

They slipped, slid, stumbled down the sandy brush-choked ravine and crawled back up to peer over the rim at the onrushing riders. Only four of them, Kendo noted. Where would the others have gone? To pursue Carla, was his first guess, but there was no telling what had occurred back at the DL, or Ambrose.

Bullets now sang through the screen of brush, clipping off twigs in their passing. The marksmen were much too good. Even from horseback their shots were close and menacing. The big white horse, still in the lead, rushed toward them. Behind it, three dark horsemen sat their mounts, no hands on the reins, levering shots through their Winchesters. It was remarkable, until Kendo reminded himself that this was the way these men made their living. Guns were their way of life, and they were superbly skilled in their use.

'Recognize them?' Kendo asked Nita. She lifted her face; there was sand on her cheek, terror in her eyes.

'No, but the lead rider. . . .' There wasn't time to listen to the rest of it. The pursuers were now within range of his handgun – the only weapon he had available – and Kendo steadied himself, his elbow against the rim of the gully and fired three shots. Two missed, the second caught a rider on a bay horse in the chest and he somersaulted backwards from his pony.

At the same moment, Darcy Pitt, unnoticed by the DL riders, opened up from the opposite side of the dogleg and he took down a second rider's horse. The animal rolled and the outlaw riding him was crushed beneath its weight.

Kendo had only three rounds remaining in the cylinder of his Colt and he waited as a man on a black horse drove down on them like a charging cavalryman and urged his horse to leap the gully. Either the horseman had misjudged the distance or his horse was too weary to make the leap. As Nita and Kendo ducked low the black's hoofs flashed briefly beside their heads and then the animal thudded headfirst into the far bank of the arroyo, snapping its neck.

The rider, dazed and confused, nevertheless rose to his knees and brought his rifle to his shoulder. Kendo, from his back against the side of the gully, triggered off first and the gunman sagged to the floor of the sandy wash, quite dead.

That left one DL henchman and Kendo scrambled back up the sandy bluff to retake his position, but the rider on the big white horse had broken off the engagement, spun his mount and was now racing away. Already he was well out of handgun range, and yet Pitt had not fired. Had they somehow spotted Darcy and in the confusion, shot him?

As the horse vanished, Kendo got his answer. Up the sandy wash, brushing the willow branches aside, Darcy Pitt appeared, unharmed. 'You all right?' Pitt said, glancing at the black horse and the sprawled DL rider.

'We're all right,' Kendo answered. Then, 'Pitt, you must have had the last man in your sights. Why didn't you fire. That was Drew Link himself?'

'No, it wasn't,' Nita said quietly. She sat on the slope, knees drawn up, dusting her face off. 'It was

Mr Link's white stallion, but it was Lonnie riding it.'

'Lonnie. . . .'

'I recognized her for a woman,' Pitt said, seating himself wearily. He wiped perspiration from his eyes. 'That's why I didn't fire, Kendo. Maybe I should have . . . but I have never killed a woman in my life, and I wasn't going to start now.'

'Hooray for chivalry,' Kendo said bitterly. After a few minutes when his temper had cooled, he placed a hand on the old plainsman's shoulder and said, 'It's all right, Darcy. Thanks for what you did do.'

They took the time to examine the casualties, but not to bury them. The man Kendo had first shot was none other than Thad Connely. Darcy Pitt's victim, Nita knew as a Missouri gunman called Szabo. The last of them, the man who had so recklessly charged them on his black was Oscar Campbell.

'That settles a few scores,' Kendo said, removing his hat to wipe his brow. 'We'll be all right now. Once we reach Pierce's, they won't dare follow. We've enough men there to fight them off.'

Darcy Pitt stood with his rifle in his hand, his long gray hair drifting in the breeze, his bandaged head lowered. He lifted his eyes to Kendo.

'You aren't thinking straight, Kendo. You are forgetting how this gang works. When the herd was taken, it was in collaboration with the DL. Back at the

Pierce Ranch we've got three men who worked with them. Chandler, McColl and Charlie Weeks. No, my friend, we will not have numbers on our side when trouble comes. And we're taking it directly to poor old Frank Pierce's doorstep.'

NINE

'What's the matter?' Nita asked, as Kendo slowed and then halted his horse in sight of the Pierce Ranch. 'I thought we were in a hurry to get this done, to warn them.'

'I don't know what kind of reception I'll get, Nita,' Kendo said, tilting his hat back. 'Frank Pierce might have been told that I stole his herd. In fact, I'm sure that's what he will have heard. And when I did not come back. . . .'

'You couldn't come back! Not with a bullet in your back,' Nita said.

'Yes, well, that's true enough, but there will have been lies told, sworn to by three old hands, and you know what they say about a lie repeated often enough.'

'Darcy knows. Shouldn't we wait for him?' Nita

said, for the injured man on the dowager mare had fallen far behind them on the trek.

'I suppose so,' Kendo answered, 'but I've wanted to face this down for a long time now. I have to clear myself with Pierce – it's very important to me. If I put it off . . . I wonder if I would not just ride away instead of facing him.'

'You wouldn't do that, Kendo,' Nita said gently, 'you're not that kind of man.'

'I need to tell you, Nita, about a place called Corn Creek.'

'Do you need to do it now, Kendo?' she said, her voice a little sharp. 'Or is it another way of delaying an unpleasant event?'

Kendo's lips twisted slightly in an expression that was neither a smile or a frown. Perhaps it signaled only unhappy determination, for he nodded and told her, 'I don't know. Anyway that story will wait. Let's go down and talk to Frank.'

Someone must have spotted the incoming riders, for, as they neared the front porch of the house, there stood Frank Pierce, leaning on a cane, his sons beside him. None of the three looked happy to see Kendo.

The expression on Kendo's face reflected uncertainty. Maybe he had made a mistake in coming back. Maybe he should have just kept on running.

'Here you are, Kendo,' Nita said quietly. 'It's got to be done – that's what you told me.'

She was right. He was tired of running, damned tired of it. He started his mount forward, riding through the shade of the big oak trees, Nita trailing just a little behind. Reaching the front porch he said to Pierce, 'We've got some talking to do, Frank.'

'You're damned right!' the old man barked. 'Four thousand dollars' worth of talking.'

Kendo and Nita hitched their horses. The eyes of the Pierce boys were trained on them all the time. Narrow, harsh eyes in boyish faces. Entering the house Kendo followed the hobbled Frank Pierce into the low-ceilinged drawing room. The floors were polished oak, the furniture dark and heavy. Pierce lowered himself into the largest chair and steepled his fingers, looking up at Kendo with savage eyes.

'All right,' he said with forced calmness, 'let's hear what you have to say for yourself, Kendo.'

Before Kendo could begin, they heard the heavy fall of bootsteps on the porch and the front door was swung wide to admit Bo Chandler and Rex McColl. They tramped across the floor, Bo Chandler's broad face expressionless but angry. McColl cast one of his scornful smiles in Kendo's direction, took a moment to let his eyes sweep over Nita and then sagged into a chair, placing his hat on his crossed knee.

'Spend that money already?' McColl asked.

'Quiet,' Frank Pierce said. 'Kendo came to talk – to make a confession, I suppose. Or have you got some story made up hoping to avoid prosecution.'

'Neither,' Kendo said calmly. He was standing near the native stone fireplace, one elbow resting on the mantel. 'I've come to accuse a couple of murdering, heartless thugs. There's more of them, but these two will do for a start. Mr Pierce, you are looking at two of the ringleaders who rustled the herd.'

'Rustled!' Bo Chandler was on his feet, indignation flushing his face. 'How can a herd be rustled when it was delivered to its proper destination? And signed for!' He looked at Frank Pierce. 'Mr Pierce has the signed receipt from Drew Link – forty-seven ponies delivered as agreed to. The money paid to you, Kendo. What are you trying to pull?'

'No money was ever paid to me, Bo,' Kendo said, straightening up. His mouth was a thin, bitter line. 'You know that. And you know that you tried to kill me, Darcy Pitt and Aaron Collier because we were honest men riding for the brand.'

'Then what did happen to the money?' Pierce asked, raising his eyes as his two sons entered and took up strategic positions in the close room. 'Tell me, Kendo.'

'Chandler, Charlie Weeks and Rex here took the herd along with a group of DL riders. They were delivered to Link, all right, but he only paid half of the money that he had agreed to. That money went into these men's pockets. A good deal for both sides – not so good for you.'

'Spins a good yarn, don't he?' Bo Chandler said, looking at McColl who only smiled and shook his head. 'This is all bull, and you know it, Mr Pierce. The man's only trying to clear his name – after he has tucked away the four-thousand dollars. He's trying to keep you from hanging him.'

'That's a lie!' Nita said forcefully. She strode forward, bracing herself in front of Frank Pierce. 'Kendo is telling the truth. They shot him down and took the herd. Drew Link paid these other men one-half of what he had agreed to pay you, so they all profited.'

There was fire in Nita's dark eyes, heat in her words. Frank Pierce studied her thoughtfully, asking quietly, 'Were you there, young lady, when the herd was taken?'

'No, but. . . .'

'Were you there when Drew Link paid for the horses?'

'I was not,' Nita said, seeming on the verge of tears. 'But. . . .'

'*I was*,' another voice put in, and heads turned toward the newcomer. No one had heard the old trailsman slip into the room, but now Darcy Pitt, filthy bandage still wrapped around his head, his tangled gray hair flowing free down his back, approached. 'At least for a part of it. I never made it to the DL because after Link's riders rode in, one of them shot me down. I saw just enough to know what was up, and they knew that. I believe Aaron Collier is dead. I know they shot Hatha dead and tried to kill Kendo.'

Rex McColl was on his feet, his face twisted with violent anger. It was Bo Chandler who was the target of his rage. 'I told you we should go back and make sure Pitt was dead!'

'Shut up!' Bo Chandler screamed. There was panic in his eyes now, and his hand dropped toward his holstered sidearm. Before he could bring it up, two shots were fired. Smoke rose from the muzzles of each of the Pierce boys' rifles.

McColl shouted, 'To hell with you, Kendo!' and drew. Kendo's Colt was quicker. He drilled Rex McColl in the chest and the badman stumbled backward, tripped over a low table and fell to the floor, dead.

For a long moment, as the gunsmoke cleared, no one spoke. It was left to Frank Pierce to break the silence. 'What now, Kendo?'

'Now, I think we have a talk with Charlie Weeks. He's bound to know where they stashed the stolen money. After he finds out that Bo and McColl are both dead, he'll probably be willing to talk.'

'I'm sorry, Kendo . . . just sorry,' Pierce managed to say without lifting his eyes. 'At least it's all over now.'

'I doubt it,' Kendo had to tell him. 'I think the DL gang will be riding this way.'

'For what possible reason? The money, you mean?'

'Partly. Although that will probably be used only to convince the DL gunmen that the ride is worth it. It's Nita they want. Or, if they haven't guessed right, they may think that Carla Link is with me. It's like this. . . .' Kendo explained it as well as he could while Frank Pierce's lined face continued to wear a confused frown.

'The DL,' Nita put in, 'is nothing more than a criminal enterprise. It has been nearly from the start. Road agents, rustlers, killers, can find safe haven there. I don't know as much as Carla about all of the workings of the dark empire, but I know enough. They don't want either of us going anywhere near the law. Certainly Lonnie Link does not. She is banking all on continuing the enterprise after her father passes away. She wants to be a wealthy and powerful woman – very wealthy. Very powerful.'

'I can't believe that Drew Link was aware of all of this. How could he have gone so wrong?' Pierce asked miserably.

'We don't know how much the old man knows,' Kendo said. 'Perhaps he only suspected. It could be that Lonnie has been in control for quite a long time. How could he bring himself to accuse his daughter?'

'I see. I think he must have known, but . . . What now, Kendo? What can we do?'

'Be ready for them, Frank. Maybe we're not a match for an outlaw band, but there's still me, Darcy, your sons. And Billy Collier?'

'Billy's healed up well enough.'

'And there's Ben Rush, he can shoot whether or not his leg's sound enough to straddle a pony. Young Dooley, Grant and Cooky who can use a scattergun if he has to. It's hardly an army, but we can put up a good fight.'

Pierce was staring straight ahead. The sunlight winked through the faded fluttering curtains. 'How many riders can the DL muster?' the old man asked.

Nita answered. 'Twenty men easily, maybe more. If Lonnie promises them they can split the two thousand – and whatever else you might have around to loot – why, a hundred dollars a man for a little job like this will have them clamoring for a chance to ride.'

'But why?' Pierce moaned. 'All because of you?' he demanded of Nita.

'If I thought that, I would ride away and leave you alone, Mr Pierce. I'm sure that what Lonnie Link wants chiefly is revenge on her sister. I hope Carla did make her escape, but I can't begin to guess whether she did or not. The trouble is that there are too many people here who know about the DL's business – me, Kendo, Darcy, and for all she knows, Bo Chandler, McColl and Charlie Weeks. That is a lot of witnesses to have running around to accuse her.

'And by now, she will know, Mr Pierce, that you also must have some knowledge of the illegal activities on the DL. If I could run away and relieve you of the burden, I would do so,' Nita said, 'but I fear it has gone far beyond that.'

'It has, hasn't it?' Frank Pierce asked dismally. With a sudden show of resolution, he rose, steadied himself on his cane and told his sons, 'Marcus, Roy, ride out and keep watch. I want to know when they're approaching. Kendo! You'd better hold a meeting in the bunkhouse. Right now . . . no,' he changed his mind, 'the first thing you do is brace Charlie Weeks. He can turn over the money and fight with us or be strung up. Explain it to him that way.'

Pierce stood in the center of the room, looking old, bitter and slightly confused. For a moment he studied the dead figures of Bo Chandler and Rex McColl. He rubbed his eyes with his fingertips and instructed Kendo, 'When the meeting's over, send a couple of the men over to clean up this mess.'

Kendo nodded his understanding and started toward the door. Pierce's voice halted him. 'Kendo . . . I'm so sorry, boy. I should have known that you wouldn't . . . I am just damned sorry.' The room was empty, lost in shadows. Only Frank Pierce remained – and Nita.

'Shouldn't you go along?' the old man asked her.

'I already know the plan,' Nita said. Her dark eyes were caught between sadness and a smile. 'I'd only be in the way. If you'll show me where the kitchen is, I could make some coffee for you. If you'd rather have a drink, tell me where you keep your whiskey.'

'You're a guest, not a servant,' Pierce said, seating himself again. The truth was his leg was never going to be the same again and he had trouble standing for even short periods of time.

'A good guest at least offers to help out,' Nita said cheerfully. Now her smile had reached her lips and Pierce nodded his gratitude.

'Are you married?' Pierce asked.

'No, sir.'

'You should be,' Frank Pierce said, and Nita's smile bent quirkily. She shook her head slightly.

'Which would you prefer?' she asked Pierce. 'Coffee or whiskey?'

Pierce laughed drily. 'I'd much prefer the one, but I'd better have the other. If you would boil some coffee for us, I'd appreciate it.'

Charlie Weeks sat in the far corner of the bunkhouse, his eyes reflecting uncertain fear. He had heard the shots from the big house as they all had, now he looked like a man ready to face down retribution, doubting that his case would stand up. Kendo crossed the long room to face him, the other men present following in his wake. Half of them believed Kendo to be a thief, the others had thought him dead.

'What do you want?' Charlie Weeks asked sourly, determined to brazen it out.

'It's not me that wants you, Charlie,' Kendo replied. 'It's Mr Pierce.'

'Oh, yeah? What's he want?'

'I suppose he wants to hang you, Charlie.'

Weeks tried to laugh, but his throat was too dry. His uncertain gaze continued to wander around the smoky interior of the bunkhouse, past the gathered men toward the door at the far end of the building.

'They won't be coming back to help you, Charlie.'

'Who?'

'Bo Chandler and Rex McColl. They're decorating Frank's floor right now. Shot dead like the lying thieves they were.'

'What's that got to do with me?' Charlie Weeks asked, coming to his feet. You had to hand it to him, Weeks had gall.

'Mr Pierce wanted me to ask you a few questions before they throw a rope over a branch on the oak tree,' Kendo replied. 'First – where is the money? He wants it back. Bo and Rex won't be needing their share, and neither will you after awhile. You might as well just surrender it.'

'I don't know what in hell you're talking about, Kendo.'

'It doesn't matter. We'll find it eventually.'

Weeks fidgeted and braced himself uneasily. The circle of men around him had drawn tighter.

'The other questions he wanted me to ask were if it was you, or one of the others who killed Hatha. . . .'

'I killed no one, you damned—!'

Kendo went on evenly as if Weeks had not spoken. 'If it was you, or one of the others who shot me; if it was you who shot Darcy Pitt; if it was you who shot down Aaron Collier.'

'Damn you, Kendo!' Charlie Weeks shouted. He

made a move then. Perhaps he was going to draw his Colt, but before he could, Billy Collier launched himself at Weeks, sending him sprawling against the plank floor of the bunkhouse.

'My brother!' Billy panted. 'You!' And Billy, his right arm still splinted, worn in a sling, pounded away at the pinned badman with his left fist, rocking Weeks's head violently with each blow.

Kendo gave him half-a-dozen punches before he said to the other gathered men, 'Pull him off, boys.'

Cooky, Grant and Dooley bent to the task, and it took all three of them to pull the enraged Billy Collier from Charlie Weeks.

Kendo bent over the battered Weeks to ask, 'Where's the money hidden, Charlie?'

'Go to hell,' Weeks said from between split lips.

'It can't be many places,' Darcy Pitt commented. 'Knowing thieves, they'd keep it close by.'

'Charlie?' Kendo asked again, but Charlie Weeks had determined not to say another word.

Young Dooley had been standing beside Charlie Weeks's bunk. Now he ventured, 'This is some damned poor stitching on this mattress, Kendo.'

'Is it, now?' Kendo asked with interest. He went to where Dooley was indicating the clumsy needlework on the tick mattress of Weeks's bunk. Charlie struggled in the arms of his captors, but was held tight. Kendo opened his pocket knife and cut away the rough stitching. He reached inside, found the heavy brown envelope and withdrew it. Counting the bills it contained, he lifted his eyes to Weeks and commented:

'Five hundred. They shorted you, Charlie.'

Charlie Weeks began to curse, kick and froth at the mouth. Finally he had to be thrown to the floor, bound with piggin strings and gagged.

'All right,' Kendo said. 'Which bunks belonged to Bo and McColl?'

Within fifteen minutes the loot from the DL conspiracy had been recovered. All but a hundred dollars. Still, it was nearly half of what was due Frank Pierce. Not enough to cover the cost of the Hereford cattle he had contracted to purchase, but enough so that maybe the trail boss would accept it as good faith money when the cattle arrived.

The rest still might be recovered – if the DL could be brought down.

After Charlie Weeks, swearing, thrashing and kicking was locked up in Cooky's pantry and Billy Collier dispatched to the big house with the money, Kendo set himself to orchestrate the daunting task of defending the ranch.

It took Kendo no more than half an hour to explain

the problem facing them to the men and to outline a plan of defense. Some of the hands were understandably nervous about the prospect of fighting a war with the DL. Young Dooley asked aloud more than once, 'How do we know they're going to come?' And while Kendo had to admit that it was only supposition, it was a strong enough supposition to make preparations only prudent.

Darcy Pitt could be relied upon, but after that. . . .

The sons of Frank Pierce were out on patrol. There was no one to relieve them. Billy Collier who had fallen into a dark mood was still handicapped by that broken arm. Ben Rush was a good enough man, but he was still hobbled from his fall from a bronc's back. Grant, of course, could not be posted as a sentry; the man's cataracts had greatly eroded his vision. And Cooky on a horse! The fat man had not been astride one in ten years.

Nevertheless this was the crew Kendo had to work with and he assigned each a position to be manned the moment the Pierce boys sounded the alarm. Every man was issued a weapon to take to his station and an extra box of cartridges. Kendo saw no reason to panic. They held a fortified position and no number of horsemen should be able to pry them from shelter. They had nothing to fear except a random shot or perhaps being burned out. That was not a great concern.

Kendo knew that the cleared land around the ranch house and bunkhouse offered a clear line of sight, and that it should be nearly impossible for a DL rider to cross the yard without being spotted – if every man remained alert.

Kendo returned to the big house, squinting into the harsh sunlight. Nothing moved across the plains, nothing within his range of vision anyway. He had re-armed himself with a Winchester and he carried it now. The door to the big house stood open. Frowning, Kendo entered.

'What is it?' Nita asked. She was standing near the kitchen door, towel over her arm, basin of water in her hands.

'Just came over to tell Frank what we have planned.'

'He can't talk to you now.'

'What do you mean?' Kendo asked angrily. 'He damned sure should talk to me now.'

'He's sick,' Nita said in a lowered voice. She inclined her head toward the open bedroom door.

'Sick? How sick?'

'I don't know. I'm not a doctor. Maybe it's just stress, maybe his old injury is just catching up to him. Maybe . . . maybe he's dying, Kendo. He's not a young man anymore.'

Kendo smothered a curse. 'What can I do to help?' he asked.

'Just save his ranch for him. For him and his sons,' Nita said.

TEN

Darcy Pitt was in the yard in front of the house, his long gray hair again tied back with a leather thong. The plainsman looked up as Kendo walked toward him.

'You look worried, Kendo. What's up?'

'Slight change of plans. You'll have to take up a position in the big house. Have Rush come over as well.'

'Then Pierce doesn't—?'

'Pierce is down, sick. Nita doesn't know how bad it is. Could be an infection in his hip, could be plain worry.'

'Sure you don't want me to go out and relieve his boys? Maybe they should be here if their father's that bad off.'

'They'd be of no use if they got too concerned

with Frank's health. Nita will tend him as well as they can. Better, probably.'

'All right. As you say, Kendo, it's your show.' Darcy was still looking toward the house. He saw the shadowy figure briefly, near the doorway. 'You sure you don't want to stay here, close to the woman?'

'I've already told you what we're going to do,' Kendo answered sharply. 'Why do you ask?'

'No reason.' Darcy shrugged and showed a row of yellowed teeth as he smiled. 'Just if a woman meant that much to me, I'd be tempted to stay close and keep watch.'

'Nita!' Kendo laughed awkwardly. 'We don't even know each other.'

'That might be,' Darcy Pitt answered, glancing toward the house again. 'But when a woman has that look in her eyes. . . .'

'What look?'

'Never mind, Kendo. When she wants you to notice it, you damn sure will. For now, I'd better go get Ben Rush. I'll set up in the parlor and give him the side window.'

Kendo nodded and started toward the barn where he meant to take a position in the hayloft at the loading window. His eyes remained fixed on the distances, waiting for the first intimation of trouble, but his thoughts remained in place, fixed on Darcy

Pitt's words. Nita? It was absurd. Sure she was a fine-looking, devoted woman. Who knew what lurked behind those dark liquid eyes? But Kendo did not think that it was deep feelings for him.

If so, so what? It was irrelevant to the day. He might not even live to see sundown if he did not keep his thoughts concentrated on the coming battle.

Clambering up the ladder to the hayloft, Kendo crossed the planking, breathing in hay dust. He flung the shutter-door wide and settled in, placing his spare box of .44.40s on the floor beside him. Then he sat cross-legged and peered from the deep shadows of the barn into the bright light of the plains' day. He had a view directly west, the direction he was assuming that the DL riders would be arriving from. True they could get clever and decide to circle north or south to try to strike unexpectedly from one of those quarters, but Kendo thought that Lonnie Link was too impetuous for tactical considerations.

No. She would rush the ranch in a wild surge, confident in their superior numbers. And she would come soon.

Tyler Morse rode moodily onward, in the thick of the mounted army. The man with the scarred lips was indifferent to the battle with the Pierce Ranch. He had even opposed it – as had the old man up to the last minute. Drew Link, his white hair in disarray, his shirt worn open, had stood on the porch of the big white house, pleading with his daughter to stop and consider, to take the time to lay out a plan, to cool her fire, but Lonnie was hearing none of it.

The woman had made her decision. Kendo, with either Nita or Carla Link, had ridden to the Pierce Ranch. They knew too much. They could bring down the DL's operations if they ever went to the law. And the DL and its enterprises were Lonnie Link's heritage. She would not allow it.

Nor could she abide a traitor.

There was cold fury in the pretty blonde's eyes, and the miles had not diminished it. Tyler Morse stayed away from her. Thad Connely who had wanted his own cut of the ranch, and perhaps wanted Lonnie Link, had followed her and had died. Big Oscar Campbell who had ridden with them out of loyalty was also dead, and Szabo, the Missouri gunman. When Lonnie had returned she paused only long enough to have her saddle shifted to a new horse, her own sorrel, and to rouse all the men who were on the ranch. She did not bother to freshen up or to change clothes. She ate on the run. If ever a woman deserved the term Fury it was Lonnie Link.

Tyler Morse had already decided that he had had enough of the DL the night that Thad Connely had roughed him up. Morse was not a bandit by nature. It was dangerous work. He had fallen into the life only because of Thad and Oscar Campbell. Men who had encouraged him. He was not riding with this army for fortune or out of love for the DL.

He was hoping for the chance to kill Kendo.

His anger at Kendo was as deep as only an irrational hatred can be. Kendo had bested him in a fist fight, split his cheek, caused Thad to berate him, but these were not the roots of his anger. It was a deep but tangible fear that Thad and Oscar Campbell had both scoffed at, but which was very real to Morse.

Corn Creek.

He was the last man alive who had robbed Kendo on that smoky-hot day. The last man alive who could be brought up on charges for it, sentenced to years in the territorial prison. And the only man who could send him there was Kendo.

Thad Connely had believed that Kendo could not know their identities. That they had been masked, that Kendo could not have attached any significance to the fact that Thad was a three-fingered man. Why then, had Kendo suddenly shown up at the DL? Kendo knew, of course he knew. Or at least he strongly suspected that these three were the Corn Creek robbers. Maybe Thad had been right, Tyler

Morse admitted that. Maybe he was making much out of sheer coincidence. But perhaps he was not. Perhaps Kendo had solved it. It wasn't a thing a man can afford to risk his life on. Twenty years in prison was an eternity.

Kendo had to be taken care of, and here was the best opportunity Tyler Morse was ever likely to have.

Once he saw Kendo dead on the ground, he would trail out, alone. To hell with the DL. It had been all right once, as a hideout, a safe refuge. Wait until that she-devil Lonnie Link took charge! Her greed would run the place into the ground, drawing too much attention to the ranch and its comings and goings. No, Morse decided, that was not for him.

He meant to see Kendo dead and then ride far into an anonymous land.

The brilliant sun was riding high, but beginning to heel over toward the western ranges. Kendo was stiff from waiting. Hay dust tickled his nose and the heat of day had caused the manure scent of the barn to intensify.

He waited.

The DL would strike before dark. Nothing was more hazardous than attacking a fortified position in the blackness of night where any trap might await, where every shadow might hold a concealed enemy.

He had heard the tales that Indians did not choose to fight at night because they feared that if killed, their spirits might not be able to find them again in the darkness. That might have been true, but it seemed to only show common sense. You cannot effectively attack an enemy you cannot see.

They would come in the hour before sunset with the brilliant dying sun at their backs when the watching marksmen were blinded by its glare.

Unless Lonnie Link was even crazier than he thought.

Maybe she was, he considered. Look at this mad pursuit – whether she still believed that Carla was with him, or she just wanted revenge against anyone who might have crossed her, it was still madness to raise an army to destroy those who offered no real threat to her evil kingdom. Even if any of her crew or she herself could ever be taken to court, what evidence was there against the DL? None. They worked in shadows and were sheltered by the wilderness. Even the theft of the Pierce horses could not be proven. And the witnesses to that bit of rustling had been dying off one by one. Lonnie, in court, smiling prettily would never have to fear conviction.

But that was not the way her mind worked. She was like some ancient warrior queen. Her impulse was to kill all who might oppose her rule.

A shame and a pity, Kendo thought, that someone so young and beautiful could shelter such a dark, devious heart. . . .

He saw two riders driving their ponies rapidly toward the ranch from the west. The pinto horse he knew by sight. The Pierce boys were coming in, and fast.

The DL was on the move.

Kendo smiled grimly and fired a single, unaimed shot into the air to alert any of the others who might not have been paying as much attention as they should have been after the long hours of peering at the harsh, empty horizon.

He levered a fresh round into the receiver of his Winchester and settled in behind the waist-high sill of the window. He could, as of yet, only see the hard-riding Pierce brothers, but there was dust rising on the horizon as if a growing storm was building. The Pierce boys hit the ground running before their ponies had come to a full stop, and they began yelling frantically.

The figures approaching from out of the dust storm took on shape and substance. The DL was here. At least a mile away still, there was no sense in firing at them, yet one over-anxious defender loosed a round in their direction from the bunkhouse.

Kendo's mouth tightened. The DL riders knew now that they were expected.

Kendo tried a rough count of the tiny dark figures and made it around fifteen men. Hard-bitten, experienced fighters they would be. Yet their toughness counted for nothing if they were pinned down by opposing fire. He tried to pick out Lonnie Link from the mass of riders, but at this distance he could not.

Ten minutes, no longer, Kendo estimated. Then the real fighting would begin. As he considered that, riders on either flank began to fan out to north and south. It would not be full frontal assault, then, nor had Kendo expected it from a band of experienced gunmen. Other Pierce men were assigned to watch the flanks. Kendo had to trust to them. For himself he settled in behind the sights of his rifle, waiting for the first rider bold enough to venture nearer.

'Dad!'

The Pierce boys, trail-dusty and sweaty, burst into the big house. They found Darcy Pitt there, rifle in his hand. Ben Rush was stationed at the side window. The panes of glass in the window where he was positioned had been broken out so that flying shards could not injure anyone inside, as had those where

Pitt stood.

'Your father's in bed,' Nita said, as she emerged from the bedroom, wiping her hands on a towel.

'What's the matter with him?'

'I don't know.'

'We need to see him,' Marcus, the older, wide-shouldered son said, starting that way. Darcy Pitt stopped him.

'There is no time for that. Take up positions at the windows. One of you should watch the back of the house – no telling where they'll be coming from. Break out the glass in the windows.'

'That glass came all the way from Denver!'

'Yes, and it can be replaced. Nothing can be done to replace your eye if you catch a sliver of glass in one.'

It was obvious that the young men didn't like being bossed around in their own house, but they yielded to the old plainsman's experience and took up defensive positions. Nita still stood with the towel in her hands, looking at Darcy with uncertain eyes.

'How long. . . ?' she asked.

'No telling. I can't guess at what their tactics might be. Could be a sudden headlong rush, could be slow encirclement, even a long siege. For now all we can do is wait, and pick them off one by one as the opportunity presents itself.' Darcy was answering

Nita, but his eyes flickered to the Pierce boys, who understood.

'I hope it don't take forever,' the boy at the front window said. 'I'd as soon get it over with.'

He was to get his wish. No sooner had he spoken then all hell broke loose. Pitt scurried to the window and knelt. Through the oaks a dozen riders were riding down on the house like men possessed. Pitt shouldered his rifle and began to pepper them with answering fire.

In the high loading-window of the barn loft Kendo had opened up as well. His first shot scored. A DL rider on a blue roan slapped at his chest and slid from the saddle, to be dragged across the yard by his mount, his boot wedged through the stirrup iron.

As Kendo switched his sights he saw a second rider fall. Someone in the house or the bunkhouse had scored a hit.

Two down, a dozen to go.

Where was Lonnie? Like Pitt, he had never shot a woman in his life, but he felt now that he could. If the evil leader of the DL could be taken out of the battle, Kendo had the feeling that the men would break and run. At least he had that hope.

But there was no sign of the blonde bandit. Maybe she had not ridden with the men, but only commissioned them. Knowing her ferocity, her determination, Kendo doubted that. He didn't spend much time speculating. He fired three times rapidly at a pair of raiders, nicked one of them, and missed the other who went to the side of his horse Indian-style to circle the ranch buildings.

The cacophony was overpowering. The layer of black powdersmoke laid down by the dozens of firing weapons hugged the ground in dark wreaths. It looked like Gettysburg out there. Riders swung away, charged on or withdrew hastily into the oaks depending on their dispositions. Someone obviously had spotted Kendo's position, for at least a dozen shots were aimed in his direction, and he went to the floor of the loft as angry lead splintered the frame of the window.

He was reluctant to rise again, knowing that he was targeted. Slithering across the hay-strewn loft, he reached the ladder and began to clamber down. His boots had no sooner touched earth than the barn doors swept open and two men afoot entered, weapons at the ready.

An off-hand shot from Kendo's rifle caught the first man full in the chest, but before he could shift his sights, the second DL rider touched off and Kendo felt the heel of his boot being torn away by a spinning .44.40 slug. That was close enough to breed caution and he leaped over the partition of the horse stall beside him, landing roughly.

There was a four-inch gap between the bottom of the partition and the earthen floor, and through that opening, Kendo could see the boots of the second gunman as he cautiously approached. It was an awkward shot for Kendo, lying on his side, but he triggered off a round and struck the DL man in the ankle. Howling, cursing, the man staggered back and then, with brute determination, came forward again, his heavy breathing a combination of pained grunts and muttered oaths. Kendo's Winchester was empty. He slid the rifle aside, slicked his Colt from its holster and waited. He dared not try to slink away, nor to rise up with the man well aware of his location. He waited. Perspiration stung his eyes. The air he breathed was composed of gunsmoke and hay dust. Peering under the partition, he could no longer see the gunman. Kendo waited, slowly thumbing back the hammer of his Colt.

The cry of success was loud in the confines of the barn. The DL rider had appeared at the end of the partition, his eyes holding triumph. He held his rifle butt to his shoulder; there was a grin on his face.

From his back, Kendo shot him dead, the bullet from his Colt tagging the DL rider in the throat. Snarling, blood gurgling in his throat, the badman fell away and flopped to the packed earth of the barn floor. Kendo rose shakily and started toward the rear door of the shelter.

The gunfire beyond the door was as fierce as ever. It sounded from all directions in an unending hellstorm. Taking a deep, slow breath, Kendo stepped out into the teeth of the storm.

ELEVEN

Running in a crouch, Kendo was spotted by two onrushing DL horsemen. He fired at one with his revolver and threw himself to the dry ground as bullets peppered the earth around him. A bullet fired from inside the house tagged one of the riders, and both turned away. Kendo waved an appreciative hand to Ben Rush who had been protecting that side of the house, rose and stumbled on toward the back door, calling out clearly, strongly so as not to be mistaken for an intruder. The bullets continued to slam into the house and the answering fire from the big house and bunkhouse formed a steady angry roar.

Nita swung open the back door and let Kendo slip through. He was about to scold her for not taking cover when the door behind him slammed open, pinning Nita behind it. Kendo froze. Lonnie Link had forced her way in, following Kendo. There was a big blue revolver in her hand, hammer thumbed back. Her blue eyes were wide and savage. Her lovely long blonde hair was twisted and tangled.

'Where is Carla!' the apparition demanded.

'Gone,' Kendo said. Behind the door that Lonnie had swung open wide, Kendo saw a slight movement. He silently commanded Nita to stay where she was, hidden and safe from Lonnie's fury.

'Kendo, did you. . . ?' It was Ben Rush's voice. He had appeared in the doorway to the front room. He had no chance. Lonnie shifted the sights of her Colt in his direction and triggered off a shot. Rush staggered back, dead on his feet.

'I asked you where my sister is,' Lonnie hissed at Kendo. 'I'll give you five seconds to tell me.'

'Lonnie, I. . . .' Again Kendo saw movement behind the door and then a slender arm reaching toward the top of the iron stove. *No,* he thought, *please don't try it, Nita*!'

Lonnie saw something in his eyes and she started to turn that way, her lips drawn back wolfishly. Nita stepped from behind the door with a black iron skillet in her hands. With all of her strength she slammed the heavy skillet against the back of Lonnie Link's skull, and the DL girl folded up to fall on her face against the plank floor, her pistol clattering free.

Darcy Pitt, drawn by Lonnie's shot now stood in the doorway near where Ben Rush lay. He looked from Kendo to Nita who had buried her face in her small hands. Kendo crouched, picked up Lonnie's revolver and checked her for vital signs – there was none.

'Dead,' he said succinctly. Nita began to cry.

'I never thought I could kill a woman either,' Nita said to Darcy Pitt. 'Or anyone. I never, never want to have to do it again!'

Then she threw herself into Kendo's arms, sobbing and shuddering. He held her close. Darcy slipped silently away. Outside the raging sounds of battle were stilling. It seemed that the DL had had enough.

Only occasional shots creased the silence of the sun-bright day outside the house. Kendo did not go to the windows to measure the outcome of the battle. He simply stood, holding the little girl with the dark hair and huge eyes close to him until the trembling ebbed and her sobs, too, settled to silence.

It was more than half an hour later that Darcy Pitt walked in with a prisoner and strong-armed Tyler Morse to the floor.

'You been looking for this man, Kendo?' Pitt said.

'No, of course not!' Frank Pierce bellowed. He was

propped up in his bed. Marcus Pierce, his arm in a sling, and his brother, Roy seated in a chair against the wall murmured agreement.

All three looked angrily at Kendo. All that he had done was explain that he had to be away for a little while – there was unfinished business in Corn Creek, and he meant to ride that way with Tyler Morse in tow. Then he had asked if Nita could stay on as a housekeeper while he was gone. Frank Pierce looked thoroughly disgusted and righteously indignant.

'Nita is our guest, not a housekeeper,' the old man said. 'She can stay on forever as a guest, but I'll not treat her as a hireling!'

Nita had entered the room from behind Kendo. Now she slipped up beside him and placed her arm under his.

'I thank you, Mr Pierce,' she said. 'You'll have to forgive Kendo. He was only trying in his clumsy way to make sure that I will be taken care of while he's gone.'

'I can't see what could be so damned important about Corn Creek!' Frank Pierce rumbled. 'When a man has a woman like Nita . . . oh, go on, Kendo. Do what you must.'

Smiling, Nita led Kendo out on to the porch. The sky was growing dark. Still crimson light was splashed against the night like distant fire above the mountain peaks.

'I wish you weren't going,' Nita said. But he had told her the story now, and she understood that he must revisit Corn Creek to clear his name with Carly Barrett who had trusted Kendo in much the same way as Frank Pierce had. He still felt that he had failed the man. Tyler Morse had agreed, under duress, to go along. The last of the surviving outlaws who had taken Barrett's money, Morse's testimony should be enough to clear Kendo once and for all. If he lived up to his bargain. Kendo thought Morse would. Just that morning Kendo had taken Morse into Frank Pierce's bedroom and explained why he had to go back to Corn Creek. Pierce's final words on the subject had been delivered with his eyes locked to those of Tyler Morse.

'If he don't go through with the bargain, Kendo, you bring him back here. We'll string him up from the old oak tree.'

The ranch now was still, the night breeze gentle as it toyed with the upper branches of the oak. Kendo turned Nita toward him and he saw then the look in her eyes that Darcy Pitt had told him to watch out for. And he kissed her.

Together they watched the last menacing glow of crimson fade from the skies, and the quiet night crept in softly, the silver stars blinking on like comforting, promising beacons.

Yes, Kendo was thinking, there is life beyond the crimson skies.